## "Which floor?"

The words stopped her short, sent her heart leaping into her mouth. How hadn't she noticed that there was someone there? If she'd known, she'd never have shot into the elevator quite so inelegantly, all breathless and giggling. She sucked in her cheeks and pivoted only to feel every scrap of her composure vaporizing. The man with his finger poised over the panel was the epitome of tall, dark and handsome. Broad shouldered, olive-skinned, slate eyed. Sad eyed. She felt her heart twisting loose, going out to him, which was weird and completely ridiculous because he was a stranger, a stranger who was looking at her with raised eyebrows, waiting for her to speak.

She swallowed hard. "Ground please. Thank you."

He nodded with what could have been the hint of a smile, then pressed the button.

She moved back against the rail, trying not to look at him, but not looking didn't mean not seeing. It was impossible not to see him because his recurring reflection was coming at her from every side.

Dear Reader,

It's been a number of years since I've spent a week in Barcelona, but the memories live on, so it was inevitable that I'd plunder the experience for a book setting sooner or later. Obviously, the romantic journey of my secret prince, Raffiel Munoz, and my reluctant aristocratic heroine, Dulcie (Lady Davenport-Brown), takes precedence over the setting, but I hope that I've provided a flavor of the city and some of its landmarks along the way.

In these COVID-raddled times, there can't be many of us who haven't experienced the loss of normal with the added prospect of an altered future, so, whilst Raffiel's journey is one into active royal life, I think his basic dilemma is highly relatable, and as a young woman trying to find her own normal, a place to fit and a "right" way to be, again, I feel Dulcie represents so many of us.

I hope you love Raffiel and Dulcie's story as much as I loved writing it. And please—if you get the chance—grab your camera and go to Barcelona. You won't regret it!

*Ella* x

# Barcelona Fling with a Secret Prince

*Ella Hayes*

———

HARLEQUIN

*Romance*

Recycling programs
for this product may
not exist in your area.

ISBN-13: 978-1-335-73702-1

Barcelona Fling with a Secret Prince

Copyright © 2023 by Ella Hayes

For questions and comments about the quality of this book, please contact us at CustomerService@Harlequin.com.

Harlequin Enterprises ULC
22 Adelaide St. West, 41st Floor
Toronto, Ontario M5H 4E3, Canada
www.Harlequin.com

Printed in U.S.A.

After ten years as a television camerawoman, **Ella Hayes** started her own photography business so that she could work around the demands of her young family. As an award-winning wedding photographer, she's documented hundreds of love stories in beautiful locations, both at home and abroad. She lives in central Scotland with her husband and two grown-up sons. She loves reading, travelling with her camera, running and great coffee.

### Books by Ella Hayes

### Harlequin Romance

*Her Brooding Scottish Heir*
*Italian Summer with the Single Dad*
*Unlocking the Tycoon's Heart*
*Tycoon's Unexpected Caribbean Fling*
*The Single Dad's Christmas Proposal*
*Their Surprise Safari Reunion*

Visit the Author Profile page at Harlequin.com.

For my mother-in-law, Gill.

# PROLOGUE

*Breaking: Dralk crash kills three
Brostovenian Royals!*

KING CARLOS MUNOZ of Brostovenia and his young-
est son Prince Hugo died when the racing car
driven by heir apparent Prince Gustav swerved
to avoid a collision then ploughed into the VIP
stand at Dralk this afternoon.

All three royals and a handful of other specta-
tors were pronounced dead at the scene.

Too stunned to make an official statement, the
royal family has requested that its privacy be re-
spected at this time.

Prince Gustav's passion for motor racing has
long been criticised by the establishment in Brostovenia, but the thirty-three-year-old Prince would
not be dissuaded from competing—encouraged,
it seems, by both King Carlos and Prince Hugo,
who were both enthusiastic motor-racing fans and
regularly attended his races.

*Prince Gustav's fiancée, Analiese Mercia, was not, on this occasion, at the trackside on account of illness. She is said to be inconsolable.*

*This triple tragedy is a devasting blow to the Brostovenian royal family and to the country. Floral tributes are already mounting along the perimeter walls of the Grand Palace at Nyardgat, where a grief-stricken populace is congregating.*

*King Carlos Munoz was well loved, as were the Princes. Prince Gustav in particular had an easy, approachable quality that, together with his good looks and unquestionable skill behind the wheel, won the hearts and minds of Brostovenians from all walks of life.*

*The question now is who will accede? King Carlos's younger brother, Prince Bassel, is next in line, but Bassel underwent heart surgery last year and, although it has been reported that the sixty-year-old Prince is recovering well, Bassel's reign may prove to be a short one if his son, Prince Raffiel, is drafted in by the royal household.*

*How that is going to suit the hitherto independent thirty-one-year-old architect Prince remains to be seen.*

# CHAPTER ONE

*Six months later...*

'It's GOOD OF you to have come, Your Highness.'

Arlo's smile was tightly framed, hesitant.

Raffiel felt a corresponding tightness notching along his jaw. Is this how things were going to be now, tension twitching behind the eyes of beloved associates who would have previously seized his hand in a vigorous smiling handshake, asking him how his flight had been or if he'd seen the match last night? Not Arlo's fault, of course. Formal condolences might have been made months ago but there was still a gaping black hole where normal life had been and everyone was trying to adjust, himself included.

He felt his gaze sliding, as it so often did these days, to the window and the freedom beyond it. Today's freedom was blue. Blue sea. Blue sky. High sun. A perfect Barcelona day, day one of the seven precious days he had left. This week, attending the annual International Conference of Architecture and Interior Design, the conference he'd founded and of which he was the patron, was going to be his last ever week of normal, his last chance to move through the world without a security detail at his shoulder, without everyone around him tripping over themselves to be correct and courteous. He felt his airways starting to constrict, something snapping inside. If this was his last week of freedom, then he absolutely wasn't going to spend it breathing stilted air with Arlo or anyone else. He needed to be himself, for his own sake, and for Arlo's.

He met his friend's gaze. 'Thanks, but I was hardly going to miss it after all the work we put in.' He held out his hand, felt a smile coming as Arlo pumped it warmly. 'And please, don't call me "Your Highness". It feels seriously weird.'

'It does…' Arlo's smile was wider now, but his eyes were sad. 'Especially after all these years…'

Four years specifically, working together on the conference programme, each year aiming for better, brainstorming ideas, ideas such as moving the whole thing to the World Trade Centre, adding the exhibition element. He'd never concealed his royal status, but he'd never invoked it either because it was irrelevant. He'd always styled himself Raffiel Munoz because that was who he was, and it was who he'd always been with

Arlo, just another architect with a passion for design in all its forms, an architect who wanted to bring creatives together once a year in Gaudí's city. An ache coiled in his chest. But now he was on a new path, which meant handing over to Arlo. It was why he was here in Arlo's suite at the Barcelona Regal, to bang another nail into the coffin of his old life.

'So...' Arlo was bouncing his palms together in that way he did when he was keen to move things along. 'How about a beer?'

'Sounds good.' Raffiel felt his limbs loosening. This was more like it, more like them. Except he wasn't following Arlo over to the fridge, was he, asking him about his latest project, or about his family? He wanted to but he didn't seem to have it in him to make small talk.

He crossed to the sofa and sank down, letting the weariness rinse through. It was how he felt all the time now—weary—how he'd been feeling ever since Dralk. That was what grief did to you. Drained you to the last drop. Even the small jumping elation of being in a hotel suite that actually felt like an interesting space wasn't enough to lift him.

'I really am so sorry, Raff.' Arlo was coming back with two beers. He handed one over then dropped onto the opposite sofa, elbows on his knees. 'I can't even begin to imagine...'

Everyone's words ran out like this, but it didn't matter because words didn't help anyway. Words didn't take away the pain. The wall of grief was towering, impenetrable, but curiously the grief itself was athletic, twisting and writhing inside, surfacing then deep diving. Impossible to contain or explain.

He forced out a smile. 'It's fine. I don't need a speech. The beer's enough.' He put the bottle to his lips and drank, which was easier than holding Arlo's gaze. That was another thing about grief. The people who cared about you were always trying to take the measure of it, out of concern, naturally, but still, it was hard to bear sometimes. He went for another mouthful then turned the bottle around in his hands, wiping off the condensation, keeping his eyes down,

Papa wouldn't approve of him drinking in the middle of the day, but then Papa didn't have a say in what he did this week. That was the deal they'd made. This week he was to honour his obligations in Barcelona, hand over the conference reins to Arlo Ferranti, then return home to a schedule of increasingly high-profile royal duties.

*The people don't know you, Raff. You need to be seen, build a public profile, otherwise when the time comes...'*

Papa's way of reminding him that the time for him to ascend was coming sooner rather than later. Time for him to step up, fill three pairs of shoes he didn't have a clue how to fill. His whole life he'd been fourth in line with the only expectation being an ever-increasing distance from the throne. Fourth in line hadn't felt like being in line at all. Fourth in line had meant freedom, a career he loved, a life that had in no way prepared him for the top job.

And now poor Papa was blaming himself for not having raised him to be more 'royal', for not equipping him, but it wasn't Papa's fault. No one could have foreseen this, and no one could change it, any more than they could fix Papa's heart. Fact was, in spite of the surgery, Papa's heart wasn't strong. If it had been, Papa would never have been handing him this burden so soon. He knew it—he did—and the part of him that was a loving, loyal son wanted to rise nobly to the challenge, rescue Papa from everything, but the other part of him, the part that had only ever known freedom, was screaming angry, full of bitterness and resentment.

But no amount of screaming could change fate. The royal household was hushing up the real state of Papa's health but beneath the surface feet were paddling hard. Plans were being laid and provisional timetables were being proposed for the abdication of King Bassel and for his own coronation.

He felt the coiling ache in his chest twisting itself into a hard knot. That meant dismantling Raff Munoz piece by piece, his architecture business, his homes in New York and Paris. He had decisions to make about which of his patronages he could maintain but the rest was out of his hands, in the name of duty. How much he wanted to be dutiful, for Papa's sake, but losing control didn't sit well, and neither did being told what to do…how he must filter into active royal life, how he must smile to order, endear himself to the nation.

He felt a prickle along his hairline, sweat breaking. Bad enough, but there was also pressure mounting for him to find a suitable bride, a bride with the right pedigree, and glamorous, of course, someone able to lift the mood of the people, divert them, because obviously diverting and uplifting the people was way more important than his own happiness!

He felt his fingers tightening around the beer bottle. As if he could even think about someone new when Brianne's sting was still lodged and throbbing beneath his skin. Five years together, thrown away just like that. They were stale, she'd said, past their sell-by date. Funny how he hadn't noticed! Funny how he'd been on the verge of proposing, literally had the ring in his pocket, the romantic date lined up…

And now proposing was exactly what the pow-ers behind the throne wanted him to do after, what, a few months of courtship with some picked-out princess? God help him, candi-dates were already being earmarked. Even poor Analiese's name had been tendered in the name of tidiness. Tidy it might be, but Analiese wasn't his type—whatever that was—and he most defi-nitely wasn't *hers*. Gus was… *Had been.* She'd been crazy for Gus, handsome, laid-back Gus… That dazzling smile of his, that ability he'd had to make everyone feel important, even *him*, the geeky cousin obsessed with buildings and art and design. Gus had always had time for him. It's why he'd loved him so much…

He felt a hot ache filling his throat. He wasn't a worthy successor. He didn't have a quarter of his cousin's charisma, not that charisma had done Gus any good in the end, had it? Charisma wasn't Teflon. He felt the ache spreading, his sinuses burning. Why did Gus have to have been hell-bent on racing no matter what? Why couldn't Uncle Carlos have been less indulgent, said no to Gus for once in his life? He'd been the King after all!

*Had been…*

He inhaled, swallowing hard. *Selfish, Raf-fiel!* Who was he to rail at his cousin? Gus had only wanted a little of what he'd always taken for granted: freedom to pursue his passion, freedom to be himself. He couldn't blame Gus for wanting that, and in his heart he didn't. But the fact remained, whether it was ignoble to think it or not, because of Gus, they were all ruined.

And now here he was wandering around inside his own head when he was supposed to be thrashing out details, handing over reins. Arlo was being kind, not hurrying him, but he needed to push himself along. He drained his beer and put the bottle down. Handing over a piece of his life, even to Arlo, was a wrench, but letting the minutes tick past was only prolonging the agony. Better to get it over with then he could hit the streets, lose himself in the crowds, maybe sink a few more beers and forget about everything, at least for a while.

Dulcie dragged her eyes away from the sparkling view and looked at both of her cousins in turn. Tilly was pretzeled in a chair, applying livid purple polish to her toenails, earbuds in, tuned out. Georgina was propped against the wide padded headboard of her king-size, tapping and scrolling on her phone, one silk chemise strap hanging off her shoulder.

'So you don't want to come?'

'Sorry, Dulce, I can't.' Georgina looked up

briefly, then went back to her phone. 'I've got a raging bloody hangover.'

Which clearly wasn't affecting her vision, or her coordination. She still seemed to be able to tap and swipe at lightning speed. Dulcie felt a sigh gathering. What was this endless fascination with phones? She didn't get it, meanwhile 'online' seemed to have become Georgie's default setting. Social media, celebrity gossip, this one and that one, doing whatever to whomever, but if this was how Georgie wanted to spend her hen week then who was she to judge? Each to her own and all that.

She bit her lips together. It was just that *she* wasn't hungover herself, and she didn't want to be sitting twiddling her thumbs waiting for Georgie to perk up and for all the other girls to emerge only to be then left dangling at the edges of things as usual.

She slid her gaze back to the view. Not Georgie's fault that she was on the outside. It was where she'd planted herself years ago, wasn't it, deliberately, because of Charlie? Charlie Prentice, the great golden pretender. *The great liar!* She swallowed hard, pushing the thought away. But in any case, she probably wouldn't have fitted in with Georgie's friends. They were light and breezy, always laughing and teasing each other, whereas she was serious, arty, singular.

Bridesmaid number five, the one Georgie had had to ask because she was family, because Lady Georgina Rayner was bound over by etiquette whether she was prepared to admit it or not, and etiquette demanded that sisters, cousins and the groom's sisters had to be invited to be attendants even if they weren't an obvious fit.

She felt a little tug inside. So maybe she hadn't always been so insular, and maybe she and Georgie *had* been close once, but in a million years she hadn't imagined that Georgie would actually *want* her to be a bridesmaid. Wrong! At Christmas, just after presents, Georgie had cornered her.

*'Look, Dulce, I know you hate all this stuff, but you've got to be there for me... You're my cousin! And I know we don't see each other a lot these days, but that's totally your fault because you never come up to London. You're always buried in that studio of yours in darkest Devon. And, while I admire your work ethic, you really do need to get out more. Circulate! Think about it. If you're a bridesmaid, you'll be noticed by everyone. You might even meet someone...someone nice...'*

Which meant someone 'suitable'. Suitable was a big thing in Georgie's world which was—admit it—her own world too. It was just that she didn't like that world very much, certainly not enough

to take an active part in it, and she definitely
wasn't looking for someone 'nice' who hailed
from it, because 'nice' didn't mean a thing, did it?
Charlie had been 'nice' after all. On the outside.

Nice lesson to have learned at fifteen, that
charm could mask a wealth of ugliness, that it
could blind a crowd, carry a crowd, turn a crowd!
She'd seen the way nastiness could hide in the
corners of polite smiles, seen the way it spread
like ink on blotting paper. It had cut her so deep,
changed her, led her to Tommy, and that had
driven a wedge right in, hadn't it? Hurt her family, which had cut her all over again, taught her
that whatever demons she was battling, hurting
family wasn't right, ever.

Looking into Georgie's face on Christmas
Day, all she could think was that this was her
beloved cousin, the one she'd shared so much of
her childhood with, and that she didn't want to be
the cause of any more hurt. Disappointment. So
she'd caved, agreed to be a bridesmaid, and then
Georgie had hit her with this whole hen-week
scenario, a week with Georgie and Tilly, and
Peter the groom's three sisters—whose names
she kept muddling up—and a bunch of Georgie's
friends who seemed to have a never-ending sup-
ply of tiresome in jokes.

They'd only been here a day, and already it
was purgatory. The thought of spending another

afternoon trying to find a toehold in the conversation was making her head throb. She wasn't interested in point-to-point, or hunting, or Henley or Ascot. She didn't want to offend anyone, least of all Georgie, but for her own sanity she *had* to escape. She just needed Georgie's permission.

She picked up her bag, toying with the strap. 'So, George, you're okay with me going out for a bit?'

'Sure.' Georgie's eyes flicked up. 'Where did you say you were going?'

She felt a little skip of excitement. 'I thought I'd try to get into La Sagrada Família, as long as the queues aren't too horrendous.'

Georgie's brow pleated. 'You mean the big warty-looking cathedral thingy?'

She held in a smile. La Sagrada Família was kind of warty-looking, but it was also intricate and captivating. It was giving her goosebumps just thinking about it.

'That's the one.'

'Well, if you think it's any good, then maybe I'll check it out later in the week when my head isn't bouncing.' Georgie pulled a sad hangover face then went back to her phone, smiling at something on the screen. 'Have fun, but please be back by five for drinks on the terrace. Saffy's lined up some jolly games apparently, then we're heading out to Opium.'

Jolly games *and* a nightclub? She bit back an expletive and bolted for the door.

The corridor was plush. Silent. She drew in a deep breath then looped her bag crosswise and set off for the lifts. If Georgie really did have a hangover after last night's champagne, then more drinking seemed sensible—*not*. As for Saffy's jolly games... She shuddered, pressed the thought flat. She wasn't going to think about that, not when Barcelona was calling, not when Gaudí's basilica was barely a mile away, waiting.

She felt a tingle. Such a stroke of luck that Georgina's godfather had recently added the Barcelona Regal to his portfolio of hotels and that he'd gifted Georgie three adjoining terrace suites on the top floor for her 'hen party', and how brilliant that Georgie had actually accepted instead of dragging them all off to Ibiza as per the original plan. Ibiza would have been intolerable, but Barcelona was the bomb. She was going to find inspiration for her ceramics here, she just knew it. Walking the same streets that Antoni Gaudí had walked, floating past Casa Batlló and Casa Milà. Today, it was La Sagrada Família, and tomorrow, if she was lucky, there'd be Parc Güell, and then the next day... But maybe that was a wish too far. Best just to think about now, the glorious, hen-free afternoon ahead.

She rounded the corner and her body jumped.

The lift was there, doors wide, a glowing pod of light and mirrors. She started to run, feeling a giggle rising, a flash of childhood memory... Princess Georgie flying ahead of her through the maze, glimpses of gold satin at every turn, escaping...like this lift...golden light...doors imminently closing...

Ridiculous, this thrill of heart-pulsing danger. There was another lift on its way, lights blinking, but she wanted this one because it was here, so close, so tantalising, like Georgie ahead of her, laughing, breathless, ready to take off again. The doors twitched and she lunged, launching herself through, feeling her laughter vibrating, shaking itself free.

'Which floor?'

Her heart stopped dead. How hadn't she noticed that there was someone there? If she had, she'd never have shot into the lift quite so inelegantly. She sucked in her cheeks and pivoted only to feel every scrap of her composure vaporising. The man with his finger poised over the panel was the epitome of tall, dark, and handsome. Broad-shouldered, olive-skinned, slate-eyed. *Sad-eyed.* She felt her heart twisting loose, going out to him, which was weird and completely ridiculous because he was a stranger, a stranger who was looking at her with raised eyebrows, waiting for her to speak.

She swallowed. 'Ground, please. Thank you.'

He nodded with what could have been the hint of a smile, then pressed the button.

She moved back against the rail, trying not to look at him, but not looking didn't mean not seeing. It was impossible not to see him because his recurring reflection was coming at her from every side. Lightly bearded, dark hair curling at his nape, blue and white striped shirt, well pressed. Immaculate navy chinos. Tan brogues, polished to the nth. He knew how to dress all right and yet he didn't exude the confidence that usually went with sartorial know-how. He was staring at the panel, his gaze somewhere else, a nervous muscle twitching just where his jaw hinged.

She looked down at her brogues. Down seemed like the safest direction, except now there was a feeling coming that he was studying her, taking her apart piece by piece. She couldn't bring herself to look up and check, but she wasn't wrong, because why else would she be feeling these little electric darts shooting along her spine, warmth spreading up her throat and into her cheeks? Why else would she be feeling so…naked? Because there was no one else here, was there, making her feel like this? Only him, and her, descending at a snail's pace in a cube just two metres by two metres.

She felt a frown coming. Actually, why was the lift going so slow? Yesterday morning, after they'd checked in, the lift had shot them up to the top floor in seconds. Georgie had even remarked on it, called it the *rocket* lift! But there was no rocket now, only this super-charged tingling awareness of *him*, this pulse-throbbing, electric feeling. What was she supposed to do with it? What could she do? Just because he was making her heart give and her knees buckle didn't mean that she was having the same effect on him, and even if she was…

She clamped her lips together. For goodness' sake, she didn't even want to be thinking about this. She wanted to be thinking about art and beauty and Gaudí, and La Sagrada Família. She wanted to be jaunting through the streets with her sunglasses on, catching the sweet oily smell of warm *churros*, not riding the slowest lift in the world with the hottest guy she'd ever seen.

And then suddenly the lights flickered, buzzing and crackling. Her heart clutched. This wasn't right. She caught the man's eye momentarily, then gripped the rail, scanning the ceiling without knowing why. It wasn't as if she knew the first thing about lifts, except that they were supposed to zip up and down silently and the lights weren't supposed to be dimming like this. Just a glitch, surely. Any second now the lights were going to brighten, and the lift was going to pick up speed, but no. No… That wasn't happening. More the opposite. She felt her stomach clenching, turning over. Oh, God! The lift was stopping. Stopping… Stopped.

# CHAPTER TWO

PERFECT! BAD ENOUGH that the girl was making his head spin, that her last-minute laughing leap into the lift had reminded him of what freedom looked and felt like, but now he was going to have to talk to her, look directly into all that sweet blonde sunshine, not that she was looking sunny at this particular moment. More nervous. The way she was holding the rail, gripping it really, as if, what? As if she thought the lift was about to drop like a stone? He felt the resistance inside relenting, warmth trickling in. At least he could reassure her about that.

He looked over. 'It's all right, you know...' Light eyes snapped to his, grey or blue, he couldn't tell, not in this light, but she was listening. 'We're not about to plummet down the shaft.'

Her chin lifted a little. 'How do you know?'

Because he was an architect. Or was he? Could he still claim to *be* an architect in this crossover period? It suddenly felt like a moral dilemma but maybe he was overthinking it. What he was didn't matter; what did was chasing away her fear.

'Because I know all about buildings and all about elevators.' Her eyes held him for a moment, and then her gaze seemed to open out, urging him on. He felt something clicking inside, as if he was slotting back into the well-worn groove of himself, the only self he knew how to be. He pointed to the logo on the control panel. 'See this name: Otis.'

She stepped closer, peering, then nodded, one eyebrow sliding up.

'Elisha Graves Otis invented the safety elevator in 1853. It's basically a ratchet system.' He felt his hands starting to move, air-drawing the system he could see in his mind. 'So the lift sits in the shaft, but it fits quite tightly against the walls. If a hoist goes slack, a leaf spring triggers that snaps into notches cut into the supporting rails on either side of the car, so the car can't fall.' He drew her back into focus, loading his gaze with reassurance. 'So you don't have to worry. We're not going to drop. It's impossible.'

For a beat she looked bemused and then she smiled, a wide cheeky smile. 'Well, I suppose if I was going to get stuck in a lift with anyone, then I picked the right person to get stuck with.'

He felt his lips twitching, a little glow starting

inside. 'Not really. The right person would have been the person who could actually fix it. I'm just a theoretician.'

'But you've put my mind at rest, so, you know, that counts for something.' She pressed her palms together. 'I'm Dulcie, by the way.'

Subtle, that pressing of the palms, signalling that a handshake wasn't necessary. Maybe she thought it was simply too weird a situation for formality, or that it would be weird for them to touch. Either way, it was fine by him. Touching her would undoubtedly trigger a surge of inappropriate heat in a certain part of his anatomy.

He smoothed his own palms together. 'Raffiel, but most people call me Raff.'

'Nice to meet you, Raff the theoretician.' And then her eyes darted to the panel. 'Speaking of which, I also have a theory, which is that we should probably be pressing an emergency button or something, so they know we're stuck.'

'They know already.'

'How?'

'It's a digital system, self-monitoring. They'll be working on it right now. It'll be fixed in no time.' Which, confusingly, was suddenly feeling like a blow because he was enjoying her company. She was intriguing, 'quaint' as the English might say.

She *was* English, definitely. She had one of

those mellow, slightly husky voices that seemed to contain a chuckle, and she had that quintessential English complexion, creamy skin, roses in her cheeks. Rosebud lips. He'd studied them earlier through the mirror when she'd been looking away. He'd got the shape down, that Cupid's bow above and the fullness below, a sweet, tantalising pout, but he needed not to be staring at her mouth right now, because he could feel heat stirring in exactly the place that he didn't want to be feeling it.

'So...' She was moving back to the rail. 'I presume you're staying here too...'

'No. Actually I'm not.' Something flickered through her gaze, but he couldn't catch it properly, not in this light. 'I was in a business meeting with an associate who's staying in one of the terrace suites.'

'Ah.' She looked down at her shoes.

Black mannish shoes, with no socks. Cropped black pants. White shirt, fitted, but not tight. Black bag, black choker with a silver hieroglyphic layered over some longer silver necklaces. A sort of urchin look, but classy somehow. Maybe it was her loosely knotted hair or the upright way she held herself that was giving her that edge. God, she was hard to pin down.

He swallowed. Why was he even trying? It wasn't as if pinning her down were important, as if he were in any kind of a place to let this flicker of interest kindle into anything whatsoever. Maybe it was just that trying to pin her down was more enjoyable than churning away about the handover speech Arlo had asked him to make at the conference's charity ball, the ball he'd inaugurated but didn't even want to attend now because it was just another thing he was losing.

But all this pondering wasn't filling in the silence, was it? The problem was what to say. She'd effectively asked him where he was staying, and he needed to give her something, but what? He wasn't exactly prepared for answering questions about himself, even the simplest ones, because nothing was simple any more.

God, he was overthinking again. It really didn't matter what he said because in a few moments the lift was going to be fixed and then they'd be going their separate ways and he was never going to see her again. He pressed his lips together. Even so, he couldn't bring himself to invent something. The truth would have to do, just not all of it.

'I'm staying at Port Vell Marina.'

'Oh.' She lifted her face, smiling. 'So you're a sailor!'

'No. I'm what you call a freeloader. It's my uncle's yacht...' or had been. Why did he keep forgetting that the royal yacht was Papa's now and that soon it would be his? Some part of him clinging to denial, blocking out the inevitable. He shrugged. 'I don't know the first thing about sailing.'

She tilted her head. 'I do. My father's always been keen on it, drilled a few things into me along the way.' Her fingers went to the hieroglyphic at her neck. 'Jibs and booms, sheets, and spinnakers and suchlike. I'm not saying that I'm ready to sail round the world single-handed or anything but I'm not a total disaster on a boat.'

'I'm sure you're not a total disaster anywhere.'

She blinked, registering faint surprise, and his heart seized. What had possessed him to say that—like that—with a completely inappropriate fondness in his voice? He'd been thinking it, but he hadn't meant to say it out loud, hadn't even noticed the words coming out until they were ricocheting in his ears. As if she had anything to worry about on the disaster front! He was the unmitigated disaster, not her.

He bit back a sigh. It was just that he thought he'd heard a note in her voice, a little dent in it, implying that she felt out of place in the world at large, and he'd wanted to smooth it away with a compliment, with some gentleness because for some reason it had felt that she could do with some, but then what did he know? Nothing at all.

He'd simply jumped in with his two left feet and now he was feeling awkward and probably she was too. He needed to take back control, steer the conversation onto level ground.

He flicked a glance at the panel then leaned back against the rail, going for a casual tone. 'So, what about you? Are you here on holiday?'

'Not exactly.' Her lips pressed into a line. 'I'm here for a hen week, you know, like an extended bachelorette party.'

He felt his eyes darting to her left hand, a reaction clearly not lost on her because suddenly she was laughing.

'It's not *my* hen party. It's my cousin Georgie who's getting married. I'm just a bridesmaid.'

The *'just'* felt like a hole he could possibly fall into. He couldn't make any more faux pas. He needed to reach for something light, neutral. What would Gustav have said? He'd have smiled, definitely, all twinkly, then he'd have said something like, Cool.

He smiled. 'Cool.'

'No!' Her eyes flew wide and then she was frowning. 'It isn't cool at all. I don't *want* to be a bridesmaid. All that flouncing about in a frock and high heels, trying not to trip or do anything undainty, being on parade, being noticed all day long, I mean, obviously not as much as the bride—thank God—but even so it's my perfect idea of hell!' She sighed then shrugged. 'But I'm stuck with it so that's that.' She sighed again, and then her gaze was tightening on his. 'You don't mind me ranting, do you?'

How could he mind? He was intrigued. Besides, listening to her bemoaning her fate was better than listening to the bleating voice inside his own head that wouldn't stop banging on about how unfortunate he was.

'Not at all.'

She licked her lips. 'And to top it all, there's this stupid hen week.' She pressed her hands to the sides of her head as if it was hurting. 'A whole week with Georgie's friends! I mean, I don't have that much in common with Georgie, but I've got even less in common with her friends. They're just… I don't know…not my kind of people. I can't think of a single thing to say to them, ever, and to be fair I'm sure they feel the same about me. For Georgie's sake I want to make nice with them, I really do, but every time I try it's as if there's a great big wall in the way.' Her hands fell and then her gaze sharpened. 'Do you ever feel like that with people?'

All the time within the royal household but that was because he wasn't used to dealing with the vast number of royal aides and secretaries and advisers that seemed to swirl about the place. What was harder to bear was the wall that seemed to be growing between him and Papa, the increasing number of conversations that contained more silence than actual words.

He felt a band tightening around his chest. They'd always used to get on so well, talking so easily about architecture and art, engineering, and design. It was Papa who'd first brought him to Barcelona when he was fourteen. He'd just been coming alive then to the idea of a career in architecture, and Papa had been with him every step of the way. They'd done La Sagrada Família, taking the lift up into the towers, marvelling at the light, at the sheer scale and audacity of the building. They'd shared the wonder, but now Papa didn't seem to be able to switch back into that gear.

Papa was preoccupied all the time with royal affairs, and he got that, he did. Papa *had* to concern himself with royal business first because he was King now, working under a weight of grief and a weight of worry about his health.

Grief. Change. So much change. It should have been a unifying force, drawing them closer, but it wasn't. His fault, not Papa's. Papa was getting on with things, embracing his new role to the best of his ability, and what was he doing? Languishing in the doldrums, feeling loss on all sides, and, yes, feeling sorry for himself. Papa needed him to be better, stronger, more courageous, but he couldn't seem to find any strength inside. If only he could make himself feel positive about the future, find the good in it somehow, convey to Papa that he was happily reconciled to the new life that was coming, then maybe things would smooth out between them, but he wasn't in that place yet, didn't know how to get there.

The sting lodged under his skin lanced him afresh. And Brianne, the one person who could have supported him through all of this, had ditched him two months before Dralk. He'd dared to hope that the tragedy would bring her running back, but it hadn't. She'd sent a tribute and a letter full of warm words but that was all. So, she really must have fallen out of love with him, or maybe it was that the new sovereign landscape around him was too much for her to even contemplate and if that was it, then how could he blame her when he was struggling with it too?

He blinked, reconnecting with Dulcie's gaze. So yes, he knew exactly what she meant, but he couldn't explain to her the nuts and bolts of how he knew, even if talking about it might give him some relief, because if he got into all the royalty stuff then a fresh wall would start growing right here in this lift and he didn't want that. Right now Dulcie thought he was a regular guy who knew about buildings and elevators, and he liked being that guy. Divulging his situation for the sake of a little mutual commiseration wasn't an option. All he could offer was a palliative.

'I think we all feel like that sometimes.'

Her eyes narrowed momentarily and then she was folding her arms, leaning back against the rail again. 'Well, that feeling is why I was escaping so gleefully.' Her eyes slid around the mirrored walls then back to his. 'Didn't get very far, did I?'

She looked so sweetly despondent that he couldn't help smiling. 'You haven't yet, but you will, very soon. I promise.'

Her gaze deepened into his, mischief gleaming behind it. 'Are you in the habit of making promises to strangers, Raff?'

'No, but you're not a stranger. You're Dulcie, which is a lovely name by the way.'

Her face stiffened slightly, and he felt his heart sinking. Why had he said that? It had sounded like a cheap chat-up line, even though he'd meant it and even though he definitely wasn't chatting her up. What was wrong with him? Why was it that the moment he wasn't focusing hard on what he was saying to her, he was saying all the wrong things, inappropriate things, things that seemed too familiar? He was going to have to work at the whole tact thing because two left feet weren't exactly desirable attributes in a future king. Meanwhile, this time at least, maybe he was going to get away with it. Her face seemed to be softening again and there was a smile tilting at the corners of her mouth.

'Actually, Dulcie's the cute version. The unabridged version is...' she squeezed her eyes shut, faking a wince '... Dulcibella.'

He said it in his head, rolling it around, liking it. Maybe he could cover his first mistake by amplifying it, going for broke. He smiled. 'Also lovely.'

Her eyes popped wide and then she was turning, giving him the side-eye. 'Are you for real or just very well brought up?'

He felt relief winding through, laughter shaking free. 'Both, I hope.'

She gave him a dubious look. 'No one thinks that Dulcibella is a lovely name, except my parents obviously, and I think even they sometimes experience moments of acute regret.'

He felt delight spangling. She had such a lovely way of talking, her voice shading from seriousness into wryness just like that, always with that spark of mischief behind her eyes, primed to ignite. It was impossible not to smile around her, impossible not to feel drawn to her. But he couldn't let himself get sucked in. A few enjoyable moments in a lift. That's all this was. Nothing more.

He arched his eyebrows. 'Going back to the reasons why you're not a stranger...'

'Oh, yes.' She folded her arms again, her eyes merry. 'Go on, then.'

'I know that you're an expert sailor—'

Frowning. 'I did not say that.'

'A reluctant bridesmaid.'

Sighing. 'Yes.'

'And I know that the last thing you wanted today was to get stuck in a lift.'

Her mouth opened and then she rocked away from the rail and moved to the opposite corner, frowning a bit, her reflection doubling, tripling, multiplying ad infinitum. Dulcie from every angle, every one of them perfect.

'Okay, so maybe you do know me pretty well.' Her eyes caught his through the mirror and then she was turning to face him, her smile suddenly hesitant. 'But you should know that while you're right about the whole getting stuck in a lift thing, it actually hasn't been the worst experience in the world...'

His heart stumbled. Those eyes. Those words. Was she trying to say that she liked being stuck with him? It seemed like it. Her expression was open, guileless. Plain speaking in the wake of his two—or was it three?—compliments, compliments that had fallen from his mouth spontaneously, also without guile.

But now, what was he supposed to say back to her? If he said that he was enjoying it too, which was the truth, then the moment would swell with expectation, demand some kind of follow through and he couldn't follow through, could he? He couldn't even ask her to go for coffee because he'd only end up liking her more than he did already and what would be the point of that? There was no mileage in this, nothing he could offer her that she would want.

For pity's sake, she didn't even want to be a bridesmaid at her cousin's wedding, so princess was out. *Queen!* His stomach clenched. And to be even having *that* thought was ridiculous! How could he, even in the most tenuous way possible, be projecting scenarios onto a girl he'd known for five minutes, a girl who, in spite of all his talk, he didn't know at all?

He felt the tightness in his stomach shifting to his chest. Because that was what he must always do now, project himself, and anyone he wanted to be close to, into a future that was inescapable. It meant being doubly mindful about actions and consequences, meant accepting that, even in this last precious week of freedom, he wasn't free at all.

He inhaled, steadying himself. Of course, there was also the possibility that he was being a massive idiot, reading meaning into her words where there wasn't any. Maybe all she was saying was that sharing a broken lift with him hadn't been so bad, which was entirely different from saying that it had been good! Maybe she was simply being polite. Yes. That had to be it. She was being polite, and he'd latched onto her words, reading into them, because, even though he couldn't do anything about it, part of him wanted to believe that she was feeling the same tug of attraction that he was feeling, that same flowing out of the spirit that was warming and uplifting. He'd grabbed at it because he was morose, and she was a breath of fresh air.

He ran his eyes over her face. So lovely. Beautiful really. And if he could see it, feel it all the way to his bones, then why not every other man on the planet? She wasn't wearing a ring, but it didn't mean she was single. *Stupid, Raffiel!* Getting all tangled up in the thought of her for nothing. The only reason she was on her own right now was because she was on a hen week, or rather she was escaping from it, but back in England there was bound to be someone in her life. *In her bed!* So, time to get a grip and breeze on through as Gustav would have done.

He looked at each wall in turn. 'You're right. It could have been so much worse. Imagine if there'd been ten of us crammed in here!'

Something changed in her face and then her

fingers went to her hair. 'Oh, God, yeah. That would have been super grim, shuffling about in here, trying not to bump shoulders.' She shuddered then smiled a smile that for once didn't quite reach her eyes. 'Doesn't bear thinking about.'

# CHAPTER THREE

DULCIE STOPPED WALKING and forced herself to savour the sight of the western bell towers reaching skywards in the company of a bright yellow crane. Ridiculous having to consciously make herself look, when looking, *seeing* Gaudí's basilica for herself was the only thing that had kept her going all morning, through all that waiting for Georgie to stir so she could ask for permission to escape.

Her heart contracted. If only she hadn't been quite so keen on escaping. If she'd been just a little less excited, a fraction less overjoyed, she'd never have leapt headlong into Raffiel's lift, would never have met him, and she wouldn't have been in this state now. Distracted. Fluttery. Giddy. And all for nothing because he hadn't seemed to register the massive hint that she'd dropped about how being stuck with him hadn't been that bad an experience. Clear enough, she'd thought, short of actually saying, Raff, I like you and I'd like to see you again, but evidently not clear enough for him. And then suddenly, before she'd had the chance to devise a different line of attack, the lights had been surging back to brightness and in a matter of seconds the doors had been opening to a pink-faced, apologetic concierge.

And then it had been goodbye, Raffiel smiling and saying that it had been nice to meet her, her saying something similar all the while screaming inside for him not to walk away, but he did walk away, striding out, not looking back, which she knew because she'd watched him until he was out of sight.

She sighed and walked on, crossing into the Plaça de la Sagrada Família. So unfair. How long was it since she'd met anyone she actually liked, more than liked? A pang unleashed itself, transforming into a deep tugging ache. This was bonkers. It felt like…like pining, as if a hole were opening up inside.

She sank down onto a vacant bench, letting the feelings resolve. She was missing him, a man she didn't even know. And yet to some inside part of herself that small detail didn't seem to matter. Even if all she knew about him was that he understood buildings and didn't know how to sail, she could feel him still, the sadness inside him, and the light too…

The problem was they'd said goodbye too quickly. No time for extricating herself from the tangle of him, for drawing a line under him in a clean, sensible way, so now it was this elastic tug straining, this wanting to be where he was, wanting to see what they could be…

She felt a frown coming. She was going mad, clearly. How could she even be thinking along those lines…*what they could be*? Raff might have said some unexpected things, some nice, complimentary sorts of things, but that didn't mean he liked her, that they could *be* anything. Obviously not, because he'd taken himself off pretty purposefully, hadn't he, without a backwards glance? That was the writing on the wall, right there. Big letters. Bold. Unequivocal. Raffiel was not interested in Dulcie.

She chewed the edge of her lip, letting the fact harden. Perhaps she'd simply fallen into the trap of easy alliance because of the situation, because when the lift had stopped and the lights had dimmed, she'd felt scared. And he'd taken her fear and wiped it all away with his glorious explanation of how lifts worked, his hands going, long fingers describing shapes in the air, his intelligent gaze all warm and intent. Reassuring. Maybe that was why she'd poured things out about herself so comfortably, because she'd felt safe with him, because Raff made her feel safe.

Poor man, having to listen to her ranting about Georgie's friends. Captive audience, literally, but he hadn't seemed to mind, and it had felt good letting it all out, admitting to her own otherness, that feeling of not belonging. She hadn't confided in anyone like that for a long time, not since Tommy, and feeling that she could, with Raff, must just have ignited something inside her, got her hoping again...

She closed her eyes. So maybe things hadn't gone the way she'd wanted them to go with Raff but if he'd been able to bring her to life, then perhaps it was a sign that she was ready to put herself out there again, *circulate*, find someone 'nice'. Someone 'suitable'.

She felt a sudden throb of nausea. Suitable like Charlie... Exuding all that well-practised charm in front of people who mattered: parents; teachers; the tennis club captain. Thrown together at the tennis club's six-week summer tuition camp, she could hardly believe it when Charlie had started talking to her, properly talking, and smiling. *Flirting!* Tow-haired Charlie, easy on the eye, brimming with confidence and athleticism.

God, how she'd been reeled in, and not only her. Her parents had adored him for years, the dashing son of their friends, Camilla and Simon Prentice. They'd been as thrilled as she was when he invited her to the Hemphill Summer Ball. At fifteen, she'd been too young to go, strictly speaking, but because it was Charlie, seventeen and 'responsible', she'd been allowed. It had meant a flouncy dress, and a corsage, shoes she could barely walk in. Sliding into the Prentices' Bentley that night she'd felt like a princess, as if she were really something...

She bit her lips hard, pushing the memory down, crushing the other trailing memories before they could loosen.

Tommy hadn't been suitable. At. All. It was why she'd liked him, why she'd pursued him so relentlessly at St Martin's, because his background was the polar opposite of her own, because he was refreshingly open, brutally frank. Yeah, he fancied her, yeah, he'd love to give her a whirl in the sack...

Tommy wasn't into etiquette and so-called propriety. What was propriety anyway? Sham and show. It had been music to her twenty-year-old ears. This was a better way to be, surely, being upfront. Honest! For all his dark, unkempt hair, tattoos and tragus piercings, Tommy was pure gold. Golden! That's what she'd thought, what she'd seen in him. She'd loved the effortless way he flung paint on canvas and created magic, and she'd loved that he didn't fall over himself trying to impress her parents.

Not like Charlie! No, Tommy wasn't a suck up. He was her badge of rebellion, a way of giving the finger to her own class and all the things she hated about it, but being with him came at a price. A long night in the cells after Tommy had got them both busted for possession at a Fulham party had shocked her parents, then alienated them.

Never mind that she'd thought the little bag Tommy had given her to *'mind'* was his habitual weed. Never mind that she'd been let off as a naïve accessory. That had been it as far as her family was concerned. Tommy was no longer welcome at Fendlesham. She'd had to pick a side then and God help her she'd picked Tommy's because he'd said he loved her, and she'd wanted to believe it.

But it got harder and harder seeing the hurt and incomprehension in her parents' eyes, because they were good people. It wasn't their fault they didn't know where her anger was coming from, wasn't their fault she'd never been able to bring herself to tell them about Charlie, about what he'd tried to do, what he'd told everyone about her afterwards. They didn't know what she'd had to live with at her smart school, why she'd 'suddenly' decided that she wanted to go to sixth form college to do A levels instead of staying on there.

They'd put it down to a teenage whim, indulged her, thank God, so she'd been able to get away with locking all the anger and resentment inside. But five years on, listening to Tommy ranting about entitlement and the landed classes, the screw that had been tightening inside ever since the night of the Hemphill Ball started reverse turning.

A year after graduating, she'd had enough of being his moll. She ditched him and moved to Devon because it was a long way from home, a long way from everything. She found a small studio space in a quiet village. The stated plan was to *focus* on her work. The private plan was to *find* herself, decide who she wanted to be. She stamped *Dulcie Brown* on the underside of her ceramic creations because Dulcie Brown was who she was in that safe little backwoods' world. But at Georgie's wedding she was going to have to be Lady Dulcibella Davenport-Brown again. She was going to have to smile and shake hands with the ones who'd passed Charlie's lies around behind their whispering hands all those years ago…

She drew Gaudí's towers back into focus. Why was she even thinking about all this? Something to do with Raffiel, feeling that connection humming again, as it had with Tommy, except that the Dulcie who'd connected with Tommy had been an angry Dulcie, a hurt Dulcie, a contrary Dulcie. The Dulcie who'd flowed out to Raff had felt real. Softer, warmer. No point to prove, no axe to grind. Just pure being.

But pure being was no good if it didn't cut both ways, and even though it had felt as if it was, it couldn't have been, could it? Because she was here, and he wasn't. She'd deluded herself, got herself in a fizz for nothing. But that was ending right now.

She pushed up off the bench, straightening her bag. She wasn't going to think about Raffiel or Charlie or Tommy any more, and she definitely wasn't going to think about the horror show that was going to be Georgie's wedding. She'd come here for Antoni Gaudí, and she was damn well going to enjoy every second of him.

She stepped out of the push and flow, lowering herself onto one of the stone benches that ran beneath the blazing stained-glass windows. She could feel a sob lodging in her chest, wanting to rise, tears budding, wanting to fall. Not what she'd been expecting, this feeling of being overwhelmed, but the light inside the basilica was divine, appropriately enough, bright white punching through glittering oval portholes, green, gold and orange pouring in, flooding the floor, splashing the mighty tree-trunk pillars.

*I am the light of the world.*

She wasn't religious but the line had been circling through her mind from the moment she'd stepped inside and felt the breath leaving her lungs. Light of the world! Was that what Gaudí had been going for when he conceived this? It felt like it, felt as if he'd been aiming to bring God right in, stage a show not a tell.

*I am the light...*

She ran her eyes around the vast vaulted space, shutting out the crowds, focusing on the structures and the feeling, that feeling of being on a forest floor with sunlight dappling through. Organic shapes. Textures. Striated bark, leafy fronds, and the light. Always the light. It was impossible not to look up, impossible not to feel humbled. Gaudí's vision, his accomplishment, even in this unfinished state was almost too moving to bear.

'Mesmerising, isn't it?'

It took a split second to register the deep velvet voice, another split second to register its familiarity, and two more split seconds for her heart to leap clear of her body. Somehow—*how?*—Raffiel was sitting at the other end of her bench, his chin lifted, his eyes trained on the ceiling as if this wasn't a great big deal. Or maybe it was just a great big deal for her, just *her* blood that was pumping warm and fast, *her* wits that were busy scattering, *her* tongue tying itself into knots.

She slid her eyes over his handsome profile, feeling her limbs unstringing. How could that even happen just by looking at someone? She bit her lips together. She couldn't let him see the effect he was having on her because he wasn't showing anything, was he? He was simply here, happily, impossibly, but cool and casual as you like, staring upwards, his broad shoulders loose, a small smile hanging on his lips.

He hadn't been this relaxed in the lift. Oh, no. He'd been kind and warm and sweet, but also a bit reined in. But of course they'd been confined then, small space, first meeting, no escape. This was different. Huge space, second meeting, plenty of exits. *Second meeting.* She felt a tingle. By chance or design?

'It is mesmerising, yes.' She took a careful breath, reaching for a casual tone. 'So, I'm sorry but…are you stalking me?'

His eyes snapped to hers. 'Last time I checked I wasn't, but it seems not to have made any difference.' And then he was angling himself towards her, smiling a smile that melted her bones. 'I wasn't sure if I should come over or not, but it seemed rude not to, after the lift, I mean.' Hesitation flickered through his gaze. 'But if you want to be alone, I'll leave you in peace, no hard feelings.'

'No! It's fine. Really.' More perfect than fine, but she wasn't going to say that to his face. She nodded towards the milling tourists. 'What I mean is that you're hardly disturbing me. Besides…' Her belly knotted. Crunch time. Did she dare spell it out for him, risk embarrassing them both? If she didn't, she'd only regret it. Maybe the thing to hold onto was that he was here, sitting on her bench. He'd made the first move, effectively, so maybe it wasn't that much of a risk. She felt a smile coming. 'Besides…it's nice to see you.'

A light came into his eyes that drew a sudden unexpected heat through her veins. She looked away quickly, heart drumming, watching a couple smiling into a phone attached to the end of a selfie stick. Was he feeling it too, this insane tug of attraction, this deep liquid ache?

'It's nice to see you too.' His voice broke through, his accent warm and seductive. Russian? German maybe? Or Swedish? European for sure. 'And lucky actually…'

*Lucky!*

She turned, meeting his gaze, which was shyer now, more like it had been in the lift. 'Lucky why?'

He faltered for a moment. 'Because after I left

you, I got to thinking that maybe I should have suggested a coffee or something, instead of dashing off...'

Her heart skipped and then it was fluttering, lifting higher and higher. He was initiating something, taking the lead, leading her exactly where she wanted to go. She could feel the air between them clearing then filling with a low electric hum. Charged air. Charged moment. It was going to be hard keeping her voice level, even harder to keep her smile neatly corralled. She took a breath. 'Coffee would have gone down very well after the trauma.'

His eyebrows slid up. 'Would it still go down well on the basis of better late than never?'

She let her smile loosen a little, felt her heart jumping like a flame as he smiled back. 'If *churros* are included then, absolutely, better late than never works for me.'

Dulcie's shoulders lifted. 'I'm sorry, Raff, but I'm embarrassed to say that I don't know anything about Brostovenia.'

Ideal, given that he didn't want to talk about his country. He wouldn't have mentioned it at all if she hadn't asked him about his accent but since she had, he'd told her the truth, because lying wasn't an option. Talking around the edges of things, on the other hand, was acceptable, at least for now while he was still catching up with himself, with this whole coffee thing. Yes, he'd approached *her*, and yes, he'd suggested it, but that didn't mean he wasn't reeling, didn't mean that, in the corner of his brain he'd dedicated to royal matters, there weren't fur and feathers flying.

'Don't apologise, and please don't be embarrassed.' He picked up his cup. 'It's not as if I'm an expert on England.'

Her eyes rounded into his. 'Oh, I can make you an expert on England in ten seconds.' Cheeky grin. 'Shakespeare, Buckingham Palace, fish and chips, the pound, Guy Fawkes, Covent Garden, Oxford, Cambridge, rain—especially on bank holidays—Blackpool Pier, Brighton Pier, Ascot, Henley, the Grand National, Wimbledon, the Downs and the Dales, Exmoor and Dartmoor, and pubs. Pubs are very important!'

*Dulcie.* Impossible not to smile when she was going full tilt, impossible not to like her more with every passing second, which was exactly what he'd known would happen if he spent more time with her. It's why he'd hurried away from the hotel just three hours ago, to escape this very fate and the complications that went with it, but it seemed fate had other ideas.

Dulcie had accused him of stalking her, but it was nostalgia pure and simple that had sent him to La Sagrada Família. In the lift, remembering that first time with Papa, how close they'd been, how secure he'd felt, how supported in his big dream to become an architect...

Those warm memories must have triggered something inside because halfway up La Rambla, churning away over Dulcie and his impending loss of freedom, he'd felt a sudden, overwhelming compulsion to go to the basilica, to lose himself in its intricate vastness, in all of its joyous overkill, to let everything it was swamp the torment out of him. And then somehow there Dulcie had been, sitting in a shaft of golden light, staring upwards with glistening eyes. He'd felt his heart bursting out of his chest, a slew of conflicting emotions. To go over, or not, to risk feeding a fire that could burn him, or, worse, that could burn her, or not.

But then watching her, witnessing her emotional connection to a building that he himself held so dear, it had seemed like a chance too. Twice Dulcie had been put in his way. Twice! Was it something he could ignore? It hadn't felt like it in that moment, or maybe he'd just been too weak, too bewitched to make himself walk away a second time. He'd suddenly wanted to know if what he'd felt flowing between them in the lift had been real or simply a flight of desperate fancy. Going over to talk to her had seemed like a neat way to sort it out.

That had been his logic, the last he'd seen or felt of it. Now everything was Dulcie, stealing his breath with her smile, making him smile with a quirk of her eyebrows, making his blood run hot with a finger at the corner of her mouth catching chocolate from the *churros*. He was done for, helpless, and right now he didn't have the strength to care.

'Do you have pubs in Brostovenia?' She was looking at him over the rim of her cup, that mischievous little spark just visible at the edge of her blue gaze.

He sipped and set his own cup down. 'No. We have café-bars.' He dragged his eyes away from hers and looked around, taking in the tables and the red awning over their heads. 'Quite similar to this, but to be honest...' and thankfully honesty was his golden ticket out of the Brostovenian hole he could feel opening up beneath him '... I don't know much about bars in Brostovenia. I went to university in the States so I'm more familiar with American bars, not that I'm a barfly or anything.'

She put her cup down, smiling. 'That's reassuring.' And then her eyes came to his, all warm and curious. 'So, what did you study, and where?'

He felt his limbs loosening. This he was happy to talk about!

'Architecture. At Cornell.'

'So *that's* how you know all about buildings. And lifts.' Her fingers moved to a stray lock, tucking it behind her ear. 'So the meeting you were having at the hotel, was it a project meeting…?' Her eyes quickened. 'Are you building something here, in Barcelona?'

His heart went limp. Seven years training, six years in practice, all for nothing because there'd be no more designing now, no more creating. It was over. He went for his cup again, sipping slowly, searching for a straight, calm line inside.

'No, sadly. It was just tying off some loose ends…to do with a conference.'

'Oh, right.' And then something resolved in her gaze. 'You mean the architecture thing at the World Trade Centre?'

His breath stopped. He'd mentioned the conference because it was the truth, because as far as he could he wanted to be truthful with her, but he hadn't expected her to know about it. He swallowed hard. Too late for back-pedalling now, but he couldn't get into the intricacies of his involvement—the royal patronage thing—because then she'd know who he was and instead of sitting here nice and easy together she was bound to start looking at him differently, treating him differently, and then everything would be ruined.

He felt his jaw tightening. Life was going to be ruined soon enough, so how could it be wrong to want this sweet little piece of normality to last a bit longer? How could it be wrong to want to downplay things when it was only so he could enjoy her company? Where was the harm? He couldn't see any. All he could see was her lovely face, the expectation in her eyes…

'Yes, that's right.' He set his cup down, shrugging, going for casual self-effacement. 'I'm one of the many backstage minions.'

'Ah! Very noble of you.' And then she smiled. 'The conference caught my eye because of the interior design exhibition…'

Interesting. And also perfect, because now he could steer the conversation away from himself. 'So is that your area, then, interior design?'

Her mouth stiffened and then she was giving him that mischievous smile he loved. 'How to put it…? I'm on the outermost fringes, in a sort of oblique way.'

'Which is to say…?'

A blush touched her cheeks. 'I'm into ceramics.'

'Which is to say…?'

Her gaze fell momentarily, then hesitant eyes came back to his. 'I'm a maker. A ceramicist. I make bowls and jugs… Although actually, no… that implies functionality…' She frowned then shrugged. 'I make wonky vessels.'

He felt a thread of affinity pulling, warmth

taking him over. It was all fitting now: that quality of otherness she had, the quirkiness of her style, that independence of spirit that had sent her fleeing from her cousin's bachelorette and, her choice of destination, La Sagrada Família. Through a shifting sea of tourists with phones and selfie sticks, before the bolt of recognition had struck, it had been her stillness that had drawn his eye, her unwavering focus, her state of being totally absorbed.

He knew that feeling well, that feeling of being lost in beauty, line, shape, that clamouring feeling of trying to receive every scrap, that feeling of not being wide enough or deep enough or tall enough to receive it all. He'd seen that in her, felt it in her in that moment, and now he knew, from her own lips. She was a creative, like him. But, unlike him, she seemed to lack confidence in her work. The use of that word 'wonky'…not wonky with intention and attitude, but wonky with a blushing apology.

He shifted his cup and rested his arms on the table, suddenly wanting to be closer to her, wanting her to feel his interest. 'Please, tell me more.'

She pushed her lips out. 'I don't know what else I can tell you.'

Obfuscating.

'Come on, Dulcie, you can't just dangle wonky vessels in front of me and not expand.'

'Expand how?'

There was a stubborn set to her mouth that was new, but he liked it, the different shades of Dulcie. He felt a smile coming. 'Well, you can start by telling me where you learned how to make your wonky vessels.'

She bit her lips. 'St Martin's, in London.'

'Kudos! It's one of the best schools in the UK, isn't it…?'

She nodded and then her fingers went to her cup, twisting it. 'I was lucky to get in—'

'Or…' he held up a finger '…and I'm only postulating wildly here because, you understand, it might have factored, it could be that you got in because you're talented.'

Her eyes held him, registering the words, and then a smile curved on her lips. 'Are you for real or just very well brought up?'

He laughed, liking that she was using the line she'd used before. 'Both, I hope.' He licked his lips, trying not to look at hers. 'Seriously, though, I know you have to be good to get in there, so you need to stop all that "I was lucky to get in" business.'

Her eyebrows ticked up. 'Are you telling me off?'

'No. I'm telling you to believe in yourself because I'm sensing that you don't, fully.'

Her brow puckered. 'It isn't that I don't believe

in myself, it's more that I'm not sure who I am.'
She blinked. 'Artistically speaking, I mean.'

'Do we ever though? Aren't we always evolv-
ing, taking in new influences? I mean look at
Gaudí. There's cohesiveness in his work, for sure,
but there's also eclecticism. He wasn't afraid to
experiment, to let his imagination run wild. I
think the moment you *find yourself* artistically
is probably the moment you start looking around
again for new things to try, things that make your
work "better", in inverted commas. So the tail-
chasing never ends.'

He felt a throb gripping his temples. Except
for him. It was all ending for him, but he wasn't
going to think about that now, not when Dulcie's
gaze was warm on his, when she seemed to be
listening.

He dipped his chin. 'Anyway, now I've given
you the pep talk, I want to see your work. Have
you got pictures on your phone?'

'Sorry, but no.' She was shaking her head. 'I'm
not big on the whole phone thing. I mean, I know
phones are brilliant and all that, but I hate the
way people are with them, eyes down all the
time, so I haven't allowed myself to get sucked
in. I call people, send the odd text, but aside from
that…' She paused and then the spark in her eyes
was back and glowing. 'But you didn't want a
sermon, did you? If you want to see pictures,

then you need to look at the web gallery Callum set up for me.'

*Callum?*

His throat went tight. How could he have forgotten that she probably had a significant someone in England? It had been uppermost in his mind just before the lift had come back to life, but for some reason he hadn't thought about it since. And now here she was, pulling out this name, to what, gently warn him that this was coffee and coffee only? He hadn't even got as far as thinking about anything beyond this moment because this moment was everything. Simply being with her across a table in Barri Gòtic, with the sun warming his back, was filling his senses to the brim, but that didn't mean he wouldn't have got to thinking about it, because how could he not want more?

He inhaled a slow breath, pushing down the crushing disappointment. Nothing to do but bear it, pretend he was fine. Fine. Chilled. Cool. He ground his jaw. Maybe he should view it as practice for when he assumed his royal duties. Smiling stoicism and all that.

He swallowed. 'So, Callum's your—'

'Godsend!' She was wide-smiling, her eyes sparkling. 'He is, truly! When I moved into my studio, he set up the Wi-Fi for me. His mum was the one who volunteered him, said he was a bit of a whizz…'

He felt a rallying sensation, his spirits picking themselves up. Suddenly this wasn't sounding like—

'She runs the village shop where I live—in a county called Devon, before you ask—and she was so right. Cal's only fifteen but he's brilliant at tech, and he's pretty handy with a camera too so we struck a deal. I paid him to set up a website and gallery for me and now I pay him to update it. Seriously, everyone should have a Callum.'

'Sounds like it.'

He pulled his phone out, trying to keep his smile on the right side of crazy ecstatic. Having a fifteen-year-old web wizard didn't exactly preclude her from having a significant other, but suddenly it was seeming less and less likely.

The way she'd laughed in the lift…*It's not my hen party. It's my cousin Georgie who's getting married!'* As if the very idea that she'd be the one getting married was ridiculous. And then there was the fact that she *had* agreed to have coffee with him, readily, and the fact that he could feel electricity shuttling between them constantly. He wasn't imagining it. Wasn't.

He opened the browser. 'So what am I searching for?'

'Dulcie Brown Ceramic Art.' She was blushing again, twisting her cup around in its saucer.

He tapped, keeping his eyes down to spare her.

The site loaded quickly. Crisp, clean, simple. Totally on point, and the pictures were... *Wow!* Her pieces were impressive. Vessels, as she'd said, with a skewed side, a dropped, or sometimes a pushed-up, jagged lip, disrupting the flow, but what he really liked was the way she'd painted asymmetrical blocks of colour onto the buff clay—blues and rust—sometimes inside, sometimes outside, sometimes both, so that it wasn't only shape that arrested the eye, but design, vibrancy.

He looked up. 'These are outstanding.'

She registered the compliment, but then she was shaking her head, giving him that cheeky smile again. 'It's kind of you to say so, but—'

'No buts, please. I'm not being kind, or polite.' Her smile zipped shut. 'I think these are wonderful. I'm getting shades of Gordon Baldwin, tiny nods to Picasso...'

Her eyes narrowed slightly and then she was sighing. 'Well, you certainly know your stuff but see now I'm worried that my work is too derivative.'

His heart sank. He'd been trying to earth his compliment by mentioning Baldwin and Picasso, not throw her into a fit of self-doubt. He tightened his gaze on hers. 'It isn't. I said "shades of" because that's all I'm seeing: shades, echoes. Nothing wrong with that. We're all porous, influenced by something. That's how art works, architecture, literature, film, everything.'

She lifted her chin, challenging. 'So you're saying originality is impossible?'

He felt his senses sitting up. He liked a good debate, and, from the looks of things, she did too, but this wasn't the right time. Rather, he wanted to focus on the derivative thing, put her mind at rest.

'In a way, yes. I mean, unless you've spent your life in a vacuum you can't avoid being influenced-slash-inspired. Maybe the real problem is that we set too much store on originality for originality's sake.' He tapped the screen back to life, scrolling through her work again. 'What I *feel* when I look at your pieces is pleasure. I like your shapes, your colours, the way you've applied the paint to some parts and not others.'

He met her gaze, feeling its warmth reaching in, turning him over. 'Your work might have its roots in Baldwin, say, but it's also wholly the product of *your* decisions… To bend the clay this way or that, to cut a piece out here, or there, and then with the colour, how much blue, how intense, how deep a rust, a black line or not, brushed or dripped.'

A smile was curving onto her lips, which was making him smile too. 'Maybe you thought long and hard about all those things, or maybe you just flew at it in a frenzy. But whatever you did, whatever you do, that's all you.'

'Which sort of defeats your original argument...'

'Does it though?' Her eyebrows slid up. 'What I'm saying is that pure originality might be impossible but that it actually doesn't matter because whatever our inspiration is, we always transform it. Other makers inspire us, but you reach for cobalt today because of the blue sky you can see through *your* window in *your* corner of the world. So what you make is the product of everything that comes together for you in that moment, shades you acknowledge and shades you don't even notice. But the end result is yours, work that's wholly you, so not derivative.'

Her cheeks dimpled. 'You talk a good talk, Raffiel. You've almost got me believing you.'

'Talking a good talk is essential in the architecture business. If you can't instil faith into your client then it doesn't matter how great your plans are, your building isn't going to get built.'

'I can see that.' And then she was reaching up, adjusting her hair, her shirt tightening momentarily across her breasts, revealing the pert outline of her nipples, a suggestion of lace. 'So if I want to look at your work, where must I go?'

He forced his eyes upwards and back to hers, feeling his skin prickling hot beneath his beard. 'New York or Paris. Or you could look at the website: RM Architecture.'

'So that's Raffiel—?'

He felt a beat of indecision. 'Munoz.'

'Raffiel Munoz…' Her head tilted. 'That has a nice ring to it, a *serious* architect kind of ring.'

'Thank you.' The two words sounded dull to his ears. Nothing he could do about it though because bleakness was seizing him again, draining the light inside. The website was still up, just. Even though he'd been turning down approaches from potential clients for the past six months, he hadn't been able to bring himself to pull the plug, in case Papa changed his mind about abdicating, but next week his web people were going to be taking down the site, disconnecting his old life, the only life he knew, the only life he wanted.

'Hey, are you okay?'

Dulcie's face slipped back into focus, concern playing over her features. He felt a tug, words straining at his tongue. Unburdening himself would feel so good, sharing his grief, all the weight he was under, but he couldn't. It would only pop their bubble and he wasn't ready for that, not yet, not when it was shimmering with rainbow colours, all light and airy.

Maybe he was being selfish, but he liked little Dulcie Brown way too much to risk losing her a second before he had to, and the truth of his situation would send her running a million miles in the opposite direction, he just knew it. He only had a few more days to be plain Raff Munoz. If he was lucky, Dulcie might want to spend some of them with him. Even if it couldn't come to anything, he couldn't make himself not want it, not now, couldn't switch off this feeling of wanting to spend time with her. At least he could be truthful about that.

'Yes, I'm fine…' He smiled, drawing in a slow breath. 'I'm just a bit nervous, that's all.'

'Nervous?' Little frown. 'Why?'

'Because I want to ask you for dinner and I'm not sure how to go about it, or if you'd even be interested.'

Her lips pressed together and then she was giving him the glinting side-eye. 'You're a disingenuous devil, aren't you?'

'Only when I'm nervous.' Might as well go for broke. 'See, I don't know if you've got someone who might not want you to have dinner with me so the whole asking thing is quite nerve-racking.'

'Hmm…' Her cheeks were dimpling. 'I can see your problem.' She scraped back a strand of hair that was blowing across her cheek. 'Would it help to know that I wouldn't have said yes to coffee if I was with someone?' And then her gaze sharpened. 'I'm assuming that if you had someone, you wouldn't be asking...'

'Correct.'

'Good.' Her expression softened again. 'I'm glad we've sorted that out.'

'So am I...' A huge, explosive kind of glad, a glad that was impossible to contain. He felt a smile breaking his face apart. 'So, about that dinner...'

The light promptly drained from her face. 'I'm sorry but I can't. It's Georgie's hen week, remember? We've already got dinner plans and then, apparently, we've got VIP tickets to Opium.' She rolled her eyes, sighing. 'It's a nightclub—'

'I know. I've seen it.' He felt a tingle . 'It's right on the beach, barely ten minutes' walk from Port Vell...'

'Where your uncle's yacht is berthed...?'

He nodded, liking the glow that was coming into her eyes, liking the way that his pulse was gathering.

Her fingers went to her cup, twisting it slowly. 'Georgie knows that nightclubs aren't my scene. She wouldn't be remotely surprised if I wanted to step out for some air at some point, maybe take myself off for a walk...'

'Which would be safer with a chaperone.'

'Definitely.' The corner of her mouth ticked up. 'Are you offering?'

'It would be remiss of me not to.'

'Okay, then.' Her breaking smile knocked the breath clean out of him. 'In that case, you'd better give me your number.'

# CHAPTER FOUR

'AT GLASTO LAST YEAR, Etienne's set was insane…'

'It *so* was. But then, Etienne's sets are always insane…'

'I'll tell you who else is *beyond* insane… I mean totally *fabulous*…'

Dulcie reached for her glass so her sleeve would ride up giving her sight of her watch. Ten to midnight. Her stomach quivered. Ten minutes to go until Etienne started his set. Ten minutes to go before they'd be abandoning the plush pink booth for the vast club downstairs. Then there'd be an obligatory ten minutes of shuffling and fist-pumping in Georgie's sightline, so that Georgie would know she was making an effort, and then, with a nice clear conscience, she was going to slip out and meet Raffiel.

She took a sip from her glass, trying to quell the fluttering inside. *Raffiel.* Slate-eyed, broad-shouldered, tall, chiselled, utterly gorgeous Raffiel. That slight olive tone to his skin that hinted at some Mediterranean gene...oh, and that accent! She sipped again, hiding her smile in her glass. So much to find out, so many things to ask. When was the last time she'd felt this excited about anyone, this curious, this tingly?

'Dulce?' Georgie was looking over, her eyes sharp. 'You okay?'

'Of course.' She loosened her smile to fit the moment. 'Great place, isn't it...?' Glassy, glitzy, lights and mirrors. Long pale bar with its rows of jewel-bright bottles. The floor beneath her feet was throbbing faintly courtesy of the support act who'd come on earlier, the support act that would be ceding to the enigmatic Etienne in T minus five minutes. Not that she was counting or anything.

'It's the best!' Georgie was smiling back, a touch of what looked like bemusement hiding at the corners of her red, glossy mouth, and then suddenly Tilly was pulling her back into the conversation.

Georgie... Always the life and soul! She looked radiant in her little red dress—*'More fun than black, darling!'*—having the time of her life with her posse, all of whom seemed to have an encyclopaedic knowledge of the club scene. Festivals.

She held in a sigh. Festivals were another topic she couldn't talk about with any degree of confidence. For sure she'd been to Glastonbury, but only once, with Tommy, and Tommy had been into the up-and-comers, the new DJs and the indie bands, and because he was always so adamant about what was worth listening to, and because she'd thought the sun shone out of him back then, she'd gone along with his choices, convincing herself that ZincTube were way superior to the main stage headliners who were, horrors, so commercial, so intolerably mainstream.

She looked down at her black lace-up pumps. She definitely wasn't mainstream. She didn't fit with these chattering sparkling girls in their clingy micro dresses and spiky heels. But right now she couldn't make herself care because of Raff. Because with Raffiel she fitted.

Foolish, probably, to be even thinking that after what, barely ten minutes with him in a lift, then a scant hour with him discussing art and creativity over coffee in the Gothic Quarter. Thinking that was jumping the gun by miles, but her mind wouldn't be told. There was this feeling inside that wouldn't go away…a giddy, tingling feeling, an alive feeling, like a little pilot light burning—a pilot light that must be leaking brightness somehow because when she'd got back to the hotel Georgie had noticed, Georgie who was always glued to her phone yet seemed to have a third all-seeing eye.

'*You're looking very glowy, Dulce...*' Eyebrows arching up. '*That cathedral must be really something...*'

'*Basilica. And yes, it is. It's fantastic. You should go.*'

'*I will.*' Head tilting over, eyes narrowing. '*I could definitely do with a little bit of whatever you've got going on.*'

'*What I've got going on is a serious case of Antoni Gaudí. He's everywhere here and he's wonderful...*'

'*Gaudí, huh?*'

She'd felt her cheeks growing warm under Georgie's forensic gaze, but she'd also felt a window of opportunity opening...

'*In fact tomorrow, if it's okay with you, I'd like to check out Parc Güell. The structures there are amazing...the pavilions...the walls...the mosaics. I'm thinking that I'll find some inspiration there for my own work.*'

'*Knock yourself out, sweetie. I don't think I'll even see the light of day tomorrow.*' Sudden deep look. '*You are remembering that we're going to Opium tonight, that it's going to be a super-late one...?*'

'*Of course I remember. Etienne, right?*'

Fake swooning. '*He's a god.*'

'*I'm sure he is, but...*' And here she'd felt another little window opening. *'You know I'll never last the whole night, right?'*

*'Dulce...'* Exaggerated scowling. *'You're not going to be a party pooper, are you...?'*

*'Probably, but I won't spoil your fun. Promise. When I've had enough, I'll just cut out and come back here. You don't have to worry about me.'*

Sighing. *'Honestly, if you weren't my cousin, I'd be putting you on the next plane home.'*

*'Well, sadly for you I am, so you're stuck with me.'*

*Georgie* had said something sweet then, about loving her to bits even though she was driving her crazy and she'd said something similar back, so they were good, except that now, suddenly, she could feel guilt itching.

She set her glass down. Was it bad of her to be slipping away to meet Raffiel? Was it a bad thing she'd done—sneaky—laying the foundations for another liaison just in case he wanted to meet tomorrow as well? She bit her lips together. It wasn't as if Parc Güell hadn't been on her wish list anyway but for some reason adding Raff to the mix was making the whole thing feel a little bit underhand. On the flipside, what was she supposed to do? Come clean, tell Georgie she'd met someone? She felt a shiver running through. There'd be an inquisition, and she wasn't ready

for that. It was too soon, too new. There was
nothing to say. *Ergo*, she couldn't say anything.

'Come on, Dulce…' A champagne-happy Tilly
was grabbing her arm, pulling her up. 'It's time!'

She made like a rag doll, letting her younger
cousin drag her round the table into Georgie's
throng and then they were all moving together
through the bar, clacking down the stairs until
they hit a bottleneck of excited, queuing clubbers.

She glanced at Tilly. If this had been *her* hen
week, and if it had been Tilly who didn't want
to spend the next four hours clubbing and drinking, if it had been Tilly saying to her that she'd
rather spend her time in Barcelona seeing the
sights instead of lying in the suite sleeping off
the night before, would *she* have minded? If Tilly
had been *her* bridesmaid, beloved, but patently
uncomfortable with the rest of the group, might
she even have felt a tiny bit relieved if Tilly had
taken herself off every now and again? As long
as she knew that Tilly was all right, that she was
truly happier going off than staying, then she'd be
okay with it. Of course she would because she'd
want Tilly to be happy, wouldn't she?

The crowd in front suddenly surged, sweeping them through the doors into the great foggy
darkness.

'Look!' Georgie clutched her arm, pointing to
the stage. 'It's *him*.'

Bent over the decks, silver light beams arcing and dipping around him, there he was, Etienne, the one they were all here for. Their god. But not hers. Hers was on his way. He'd be outside waiting for her in ten minutes.

Ten.

Minutes.

She felt a fresh flutter starting, morphing into the low driving pulse that was filling the space, thrumming, driving, building. She started moving, finding the rhythm. She caught Georgie's eye, felt a smile coming, conviction winding through her veins. If she wouldn't think Tilly was bad for wanting to go off on her own, then why would Georgie think that about her? It wasn't as if Georgie didn't know her feelings about this hen week, and it wasn't as if Georgie didn't know that the saving grace of it, for her, was Barcelona itself, and Gaudí. Georgie just didn't need to know quite yet that fate seemed to have thrown her an extra saving grace in the form of a seriously hot architect.

Raffiel leaned against the promenade rail, running his eyes over the crowd queuing to get into Opium. High spirits. Bright clothes. *Skimpy.* A small knot tightened in his chest. Would Dulcie appear wearing a dress that was cut away all over, showing more skin than fabric? For some reason the thought of it didn't sit well, not that it was any of his business how she dressed. He wasn't her keeper. He wasn't her anything. *Yet.*

He turned to look along the busy boardwalk. People, palm trees, starlit sky. *Yet.* Such a small word but pivotal. Crucial. But crucial how? What was he hoping for, what was he after, waiting here outside this club with his heart drumming and tingles shooting through his veins? Company, friendship, love everlasting, or was this about sex?

He drew in a slow breath. Of course it was about sex. Dulcie was gorgeous. He'd have to be a eunuch not to want her, but there was so much more going on than physical attraction. He just couldn't bring it all into proper focus, give it shape, purpose.

He bit back a sigh. It was his modus, wasn't it? Wanting to draw straight lines between things, visualising, seeing the big picture, but there wasn't a big picture here, no straight lines. Randomness seemed to be the order of the day. Dulcie, in the lift, then somehow at the basilica, and he'd decided to jump in, embrace chance, because this was his last ever week of freedom, but still it seemed that he couldn't switch off the side of him that liked neat lines, prescribed shapes.

*Ironic!* In no time at all his entire life was going to be prescribed, sandwiched between endless straight lines. A timetabled existence. He blew out the sigh he'd been holding in. With that in mind, he needed to stop all this overthinking and force himself to simply be in the moment, to let this thing with Dulcie evolve, or not, according to the rules of randomness.

'There you are!'

His heart jumped, then skipped. She was standing in front of him, clutching a small black bag, smiling that cheeky smile of hers. Her hair was down, grazing the shoulders of her pale soft shirt. Black pants, soft leather pumps, also black. She was clearly a monochrome kind of girl, except for her lips which were red and dewy and perfect for kissing.

He pressed the thought flat and smiled. 'And there *you* are, right on time.'

Her eyes widened into his. 'A miracle, to be honest, because it's heaving in there.' And then she was miming a karate sequence. 'I literally had to fight my way out.'

He chuckled. 'I'm sure you were terrifying.'

She laughed a little and then her gaze slid away. 'I can be if needs be.'

He felt a frown coming. There was a dark shade in her tone, a hard edge along it that he couldn't ignore. 'So you're a self-defence expert?'

'I am.' Her eyes came back to his, a little bit merry but also a little bit steely. 'Does that bother you?'

'Why should it bother me? I think it's great.'

Except that it seemed as if she might have learned self-defence because of something that had happened, and he couldn't make himself not be bothered about that. If he were to ask her about it, would it tarnish the mood? Maybe, but then again, she was the one who'd slanted her voice darkly when she needn't have, when she could simply have breezed past it.

He searched her gaze. Was she trying to open a door? Did she *want* to talk about it? He could throw her an opening, just in case, and if she batted it away then he'd leave it. For now. He took a breath. 'The only thing is that I'm sensing you learned for a reason...'

Her eyebrows slid upwards. 'Intuitive Jedi you are.'

Doing a Yoda voice to what, soften the confirmation? Suddenly it didn't feel like a subject to be talking about outside the club. He straightened, motioning for her to walk with him, feeling his belly hardening, his fists wanting to clench. The thought of anyone—*anyone*—trying to hurt Dulcie was making his blood boil.

He swallowed hard. 'Do you want to get a drink somewhere?'

'Maybe, in a while.' She looped her bag over her head, poking her arm through, and then she was lifting up her hair, shaking it out, powdering the air with a little burst of floral scent. 'Righ now I'm just glad to be outside…' Cheeky smile. 'And of course it goes without saying that the company is a bonus.'

He felt his heart warming. She was such a treat, so sweet, so funny. Which only made the thought of someone wanting to hurt her even more unbearable. He couldn't let it go.

'So, forgive me if I'm speaking out of turn, but about the self-defence thing, if you don't mind, I want to know what's behind it.'

Her face stiffened a little and then she drew in a short breath. 'It was a long time ago, Raff, and actually, nothing happened.'

'But it left a mark?'

Her shoulders lifted into a shrug. 'I suppose.' And then a funny little smile twitched onto her lips. 'You know, I've never talked about it to any-one before…' The thought seemed to occupy her for a moment and then suddenly she was cutting across him, walking to the edge of the board-walk, sitting herself down.

His heart sank. Talk about misjudging a situation.

He went after her, dropping down beside her. 'I'm sorry. I didn't mean to pry. It's none of my business…'

'You don't have to apologise…' She scooped up a handful of sand, letting it stream through her fingers and then suddenly her eyes lifted to his, her gaze level. 'I was fifteen when it happened.'

He felt his insides twisting, fury thickening in his throat. Fifteen. It wasn't a stretch to imagine her at that age because there was something endearingly *gamine* about her even now at— what?—twenty-six, twenty-seven? She couldn't be more than that. He drew in a careful breath, trying to keep his tone even. 'What happened…?'

Her mouth drew tight. 'A boy I liked a lot, a *"very nice"* boy whom my parents thoroughly approved of, escorted me to a summer ball, plied me with fizz and then, in a tucked-away little summer house, tried to—' something retreated in her gaze '—you know.'

His heart lurched. 'He tried to rape you?'

Her eyebrows flickered. 'See, that's a grey area because it didn't get that far.' She swallowed. 'I kneed him hard, left him howling.'

Admiration flared. 'Good for you.' And then the thing she'd said before came back. He went cold inside. 'You didn't tell anyone…'

'No.' She dropped her gaze, scooping up sand again.

He searched her downturned face. Why hadn't she? It didn't make sense but asking didn't feel right. It would be putting *her* on the spot when *she* was the victim, the one who'd had to go through it. Best to let her tell it, if she wanted to, which maybe she did, because suddenly she was drawing a breath, rubbing her hands clean…

'I didn't tell anyone because afterwards I started feeling unsure…wondering if maybe I overreacted.' Her eyes came to his. 'The thing is, our parents were good friends and it's such a whopping accusation to make… I wanted to be clear in my mind… So I went over and over it but then the more I did, the more it seemed to me that it was partly my fault…'

He felt words rising and bit them back hard. Interrupting because of his own seething anger wouldn't help Dulcie. What would help was giving her this safe space to talk about it.

She was shaking her head now. 'Charlie was my first proper date. I liked him. I'd been flirting with him for weeks at this tennis coaching thing we were doing. When he asked me to the ball I was over the moon because it meant he liked me too. And, yes, he did give me champagne, but I took it every time, drank it down. And when he suggested going for a walk in the garden, I didn't hesitate, and when he led me into the summer house, I went willingly…gladly. I thought he was going to kiss me, was hoping he would. And he did, and it was nice—completely lovely—until it wasn't…' A frown ghosted over her features. 'But, see, he'd been drinking too, a lot, and what kept running through my mind afterwards was that maybe all he'd intended to do was kiss me but because of the drink, once we started, he couldn't stop—'

'Dulcie!' He didn't mean to cut in but listening to her making excuses for this boy was suddenly too much to bear. 'You weren't overreacting. What he tried to do was wrong, period.'

Her gaze sharpened. 'Oh, I know that now, believe me, but at the time I was full of doubt, scared of causing a ruckus, worried about upsetting our families. Stupid, in light of—' Her lips clamped shut suddenly and then she was turning away, staring at the black shifting sea. 'Anyway, it's ancient history now...'

So was his La Sagrada Família trip with Papa, but the memories were still bright, always would be. Her memories of Charlie would keep burning as well—darkly—unless she could deal with the part she wasn't talking about. He wanted to know about that part, the part that had zipped her into this sudden silence, but pushing her wasn't an option. She was clearly done talking about it.

And then somehow, she was smiling again, turning to him with mischief in her eyes. 'So anyway, that's why I decided to take self-defence classes and the classes are why I can be utterly terrifying if needs be.'

In spite of himself he couldn't hold in a smile.

He could picture her sailing through the air,
poised to strike, pale hair streaming behind.

She bumped his shoulder. 'Are you laughing
at me?'

'I wouldn't dare.'

'Hmm.' She was giving him the side-eye, and
then she was getting to her feet. 'So, I'm thinking
that I'd quite like to see your yacht now.'

Which was really Papa's and was going to be
his soon, none of which he wanted to tell her
right now.

He got up, stamping his feet to get the sand
off. 'My uncle's yacht, you mean.'

'Oh, right. Of course.' And then her voice
dipped. 'Is he actually on board? Because I
wouldn't want to intrude or anything.

The valves in his heart constricted sharply.
'No. He isn't. It's just me, and the staff.'

'You mean the crew…?'

And then suddenly the tightness was loosening. In the lift, she'd assumed that his yacht was
a sailing yacht, hadn't she? And he hadn't cor-
rected her because it hadn't felt important, but
now…now it seemed that there was an opportunity for a little fun.

'Of course, yes.' He slapped his head, shrugged.
'Like I said before, I don't know the first thing
about sailing.'

# CHAPTER FIVE

SHE LOOKED AHEAD, registering nothing.

*'I can be if needs be...'*

Why had she framed her response to Raffiel's remark about her being *terrifying* in such a way that he could only have picked up on it? Had she even framed it as such, thought about it? *No.* The words had simply arrived wrapped in a cryptic tone, as if she'd been angling to talk about it, but she hadn't. Why in the world would she want to spend a single second of her time with Raffiel talking about Charlie fricking Prentice? It was like in the lift, suddenly spilling out all that stuff about not being able to talk to Georgie's friends. What was it about Raff that drew out all the things she usually kept locked up? She shot him a glance. Was it simply that he was a stranger from a different country with no connection to her circle?

She looked down, watching their feet striking the salt-bleached planks. *No.* That wasn't it. She

met strangers all the time and managed perfectly
well not to burden them with her secrets, her in-
nermost thoughts. There was something else at
play here, something particular to Raffiel.

'Dulcie!'

His urgent shout split the air.

She froze, barely glimpsing the cyclist barrel-
ling towards her before she was being lassoed
sideways into the broad shelter of Raffiel's chest.

The cyclist whipped past, trailing words. *Ho
sento, senyoreta. Ho sento.*

'I'll give *him* sorry!' Raff's voice was hard-
edged, his focus trained on the escaping cyclist,
and then he seemed to come back to himself, noticing she was there. 'Are you okay?'

How could she not be, cocooned in his arms
like this, breathing in his warm clean scent?

'Yes, thanks to you. I can't believe I didn't
see him.'

'I can...' His eyes were moving over her face,
a slow study, as if he was trying to satisfy himself that she really was unharmed. 'He was on
his phone, weaving about like an idiot. It's why
he didn't see you.'

She felt her pulse gathering. She liked the way
he was looking at her, the way his gaze was lingering on her mouth. And she liked the quick
way he'd pulled her to safety, that whole protective aura he had, that sense of innate strength,

not just physical, but of character. It was intoxicating, irresistible…

Her heart missed. That was it! That protective aura he had… *That* was the particular thing about him, the compelling thing that drew her, the thing she wanted to believe in. *Trust*… Was *that* why some inner part of her psyche had engineered a way into the Charlie story, to see Raff's reaction, because his reaction would show her something of the man he was? Maybe…

She searched his face, his eyes. He seemed every inch the gentleman, but so had Charlie. As for Tommy, part of his appeal was that he'd never pretended to be a gentleman, but deep down she'd hoped he'd come through for her sake, for the love of her.

Charlie: fail.

Tommy: epic fail.

Was Raff just another fail waiting to happen? He might be giving her tingles in all the right places, but he was also making her act out of character: a midnight date at Georgie's expense when, admit it, tomorrow would have been more proper, less obvious! Maybe her subconscious was kicking in to protect her, had got her taking Raff to her darkest place to test him, measure him. It was self-defence all over again, just a different kind.

'Ready to walk on?' He was smiling suddenly, putting her away from him with gentle hands.

'Absolutely…' She tugged her bag straight, using the nanosecond it took to collect herself. 'Happily, I'm still fully functional.'

On one level anyway… Walking and talking she could manage, all along the boardwalk and on until they were at the marina, keeping pace with Raff's conversation about Barcelona, how much he loved it, crazy cyclists aside, but her mind was still whirring. If, unwittingly, she'd been testing Raff, then had he passed?

She flicked him a glance, catching his smile, feeling a smile of her own unfurling, warmth running through her veins. *Yes.* With flying colours. Sitting there with him on the boardwalk, feeling the firm warmth of his arm radiating through the fabric of his shirt, she'd felt protectiveness coming off him in huge primal waves.

It was why she'd had to draw a line, stop herself from telling him the rest about Charlie because the rest would only have stirred him up more, would only have made his fury pulse all the harder, and that would have been too much to take. Too intense. Too damn seductive!

It's why she'd forced herself to her feet, to insert some distance between them, and it was why she'd suggested the yacht, to change the subject, to give herself some breathing space, but then the cyclist had arrived, and Raff had filled that space right up, stealing her breath away all over again and very soon, he was saying, they'd be at the yacht, and then what…?

Her heart stumbled. What kind of signal was she sending, meeting him at midnight, suggesting the yacht, asking if his uncle was on board…? On the other hand, it was *Raff* who'd initially mentioned that Port Vell was close to Opium. She'd just picked up the baton, hadn't she, and now they were both running with it, but running where? Towards what?

*Gah!* Maybe she was overthinking it. They'd only met twelve hours ago, and they liked each other, clearly. Maybe that was the only thing that mattered, the mutual liking, this happy feeling of connection.

'Here we are…' Raff was stopping, sweeping his arm out.

'Here…' She felt the word dying in her mouth, her mouth falling open. The vessel in front of them was vast. Not a sailing yacht for weekend jaunts but a sleek superyacht. Seventy-five metres at least with three decks—or was it four?—brightly lit. This was serious billionaire territory and Raffiel was what? A working architect, successfully, clearly, but surely if his family was in the billionaire bracket—so conspicuously so—then he wouldn't be working, wouldn't have to.

Unless he wanted to, which maybe he did. She zipped her lips back together. Anything was possible, but… *No!* This had to be a wind-up, Raff having a little fun.

She turned to look at him. Definitely a wind-up. His lips were twitching, and there was a playful gleam in his eye.

She arched her eyebrows at him. 'Really…? This one?'

He nodded, the mischief in his eyes suddenly fading. 'Yes.'

He was serious, *actually* serious. She flicked a glance at the gleaming hull then met his gaze again, trying to ignore the dark flutter that was starting in her belly. 'What did you say your uncle did?'

He seemed to falter, and then he pushed a hand through his hair. 'I didn't.'

Instantly, uncharitable mafia kind of thoughts flew in, but she couldn't help it. Fact was, it *was* a really huge yacht. Dauntingly expensive.

She drew in a careful breath. 'Raff, is your uncle some sort of oligarch?'

'No!'

Emphatic. Spontaneous. Which had to mean he was telling the truth. She felt relief skipping through her veins.

He turned a little, motioning across the water

to the opposite quay. 'Those megayachts over there belong to the oligarchs, or so I've been told.'

'Right.' She ran her eyes over Raffiel's uncle's boat again. 'So what *does* your uncle do?'

For a moment he was silent and then he took an audible breath. 'He's... He worked for the royal household...' A familiar sadness was filling his gaze, the same sadness that had tugged her heart out in the lift. 'He was a high-up.'

'I see.' It seemed like the right thing to say even though she didn't quite see anything. The size of the yacht certainly befitted a high-ranking royal servant but what did 'high-up' actually mean? And what about that 'was' Raff had slipped in? She wanted to ask him about it, but the pain in his eyes seemed to be connected to it and she didn't want to bring it to the surface again, especially now that his expression was softening.

'So, do you want to come aboard?'

She looked past him to the lower aft deck. Open, luxuriously appointed, bathed in golden light. Beyond inviting! And so was he, standing there at the foot of the gangplank in his white linen shirt, his hair lifting in the slight breeze. His stance was open. Relaxed. No expectation in his eyes, only the question he'd asked. She felt warmth rippling through. He'd brought her here because she'd asked him to, but he wasn't assuming she wanted to board. He was *asking* her. She liked that. It felt respectful. Safe.

She looked at the interior again, feeling her curiosity stirring, a smile rising inside. 'Well, since you're twisting my arm…'

It was impossible not to gawp. At everything. Pale sofas. Pale decking. Brushed steel, brilliant chrome. Downlighters, uplighters, inset spots throwing curved yellow pools over the steps. Luxury cabin after luxury cabin, sleek bathrooms, staterooms, cinema, gym, pool, a vast state-of-the-art kitchen that had nothing of the galley about it. Understated elegance bordering on the cool and neutral, but the warmth in Raffiel's amused smile as he'd toured her around had been more than enough to offset that. And now there was this, this view from the upper deck, Barcelona glowing bright against the inky sky.

She pressed herself against the rail. 'If this were my boat, I think I'd spend all my time up here.'

Suddenly he was beside her, rolling his sleeves back, resting thick tanned forearms on the polished wood. 'So you like being high?'

She forced her eyes upwards to meet his. 'I like a nice view.'

'So do I…' His gaze held her fast, glowing, sending an electric tingle up her spine. She could feel a low liquid ache starting, her heart thudding in her throat. He was so handsome it hurt. A proper grown-up man with broad shoulders and unfathomable depths behind his eyes, not like Charlie the grabby-handed boy, or like Tommy, gangly in his skinny jeans and Docs. Raffiel was in a class of his own.

He turned to the view momentarily, and then his eyes came back. 'Would you like a drink?'

Something to crack the tension apart. Probably a good idea, even though alcohol wasn't the thing she was craving.

'That would be lovely, thank you.'

He straightened, motioning to an ice bucket that had somehow appeared on the low table in the seating area. 'We seem to have champagne.' One eyebrow lifted. 'Will that do?'

She couldn't hold in a smile. 'Very nicely.'

She followed him to the sofas, watching his forearms as he twisted the bottle around the cork until it popped. And then he was pouring, laughing as the champagne frothed up over the rims of the flutes.

His eyes flicked up. 'Does it show that I'm more of a beer drinker?'

She felt warmth surging in. He was so natural, so easy to be with. 'It only went pear-shaped at the end there. Your uncorking procedure was totally on point.'

He flattened a hand to his chest. 'That means so much. Thank you.' And then he was chuckling again, handing her a glass. 'Shall we sit?'

'Sure.' She lowered herself onto one of the pale sofas.

He took a spot beside her, but on the adjacent sofa, then raised his glass. 'Here's to faulty lifts.'

She felt heat rising, tingling in her cheeks. His eyes were saying that he was pleased they'd met, pleased she was here. Could he read pleasure in her eyes too, flowing back, because it was what she was feeling, pleasure, and a thrumming anticipation. She touched her glass to his, holding his gaze tight so he'd know. 'To faulty lifts.'

He smiled a slow warm smile, which set off more tingling.

So much for cracking the tension apart. It was back with a vengeance, winding tighter, pulsing through the air.

*Too much.*

She broke away from his gaze, heart drumming, and looked around, trying to tune in to the calming lap of the water below. Dark water, dark sky, and in between, this open deck, all pale and perfect. She swallowed a sip of champagne. She'd been on some nice boats in some lovely locations, but this was definitely the grandest. The grandest and the saddest, somehow. It wasn't just that Raffiel was the only occupant but that it was so utterly pristine… *No.* She felt a frown coming. It was more than that. It was denuded. No personal mementoes, no photographs. It was like a ghost ship.

'What are you thinking so hard about, Dulcie Brown?'

She felt the dark velvet accent tugging at more than just her attention.

She took a breath and turned to look at him. His gaze was warm, open, a smile hiding inside it. If she were to tell him what she was thinking, then that smile would undoubtedly fade. Did she want to risk that, risk bringing his sadness back?

He tilted his head over a little, prompting. Her heart thumped a thick beat. Did she have a choice though, because whatever this was that they were doing—*starting*—be it a friendship or a holiday fling or who knew what, skirting around things, avoiding awkward truths was never a good idea.

If she'd told her parents the truth about Charlie instead of telling them that she'd simply 'gone off him' after that first date, then how different might her life have been? She bit the inside of her cheek. But it was more than that even. She liked Raff, liked him far too much not to want to know everything about him. If something was grieving him, then that thing was as much a part of him as his handsome face and his thick forearms and his heart-stopping smile so how could she not want to know what it was? The problem was how to lead him to it…

She took a sip from her glass, considering, then set it down. 'I was just thinking that this boat feels very empty.'

'Well, it is. It's just you and me, plus the twenty staff and crew obviously.' A wry smile curved on his lips. 'It's practically the *Marie Celeste*.'

She took a breath. 'I didn't quite mean that.'

His eyebrows flickered faintly.

'What I was thinking is that there's nothing here to show that it belongs to anyone… I mean, it's your uncle's yacht, right, but there are no family photographs in the cabins, no personal effects anywhere…'

His expression was altering, solidifying.

She swallowed, not wanting to push, but also wanting to know, needing to. 'I was just wondering why that was. Wondering about your uncle really…'

Was she going too far? Raff's face was growing more and more masklike, but that could only mean that the pain inside him was on the rise again and that he was trying to hold it back, keep it inside. Maybe it was wrong, but the resistance in him was only making it feel all the more imperative to break through because the thought of him hurting alone was too much to bear.

In textbook terms he was a stranger, yes, but for

some reason it didn't feel like that. The strange-
ness was nothing to this deep feeling of connection, this flame of fellow feeling. Whatever pain
he was feeling, she wanted to share in it, help him,
bolster him if she could. But to do that, it meant
pushing him all the way over the line.

She drew in a careful breath, tightening her
gaze on his. 'I know it's none of my business,
but I just can't help wondering why you look so
sad whenever you mention him.'

His pulse was going hard, jack hammering.
Could she see it, sense it? Of course she could.
He'd felt it in her from the start, from that first
moment in the lift. Empathy behind her eyes
that had simply flowed out and reached in, laying him bare. For a piece of a second, he hadn't
liked that feeling of being exposed but then the
lift had stopped, and everything had changed.
Her hand on the rail, her wide scared eyes. Impossible not to drop his resistance. Impossible
not to succumb.

That was the thing about Dulcie, wasn't it? The
irresistible pull of her, and it had nothing to do
with her sweet lips and her big eyes and her neat
lithe body. It was greater. Deeper. It was the thing
that had impelled his feet in her direction at La
Sagrada Família, the thing that had impelled him
to mention the proximity of Port Vell to Opium,

hope beating in his heart for exactly this, a late-night rendezvous, because waiting sensibly for tomorrow hadn't even occurred to him. That's how caught up he was, how beguiled. And now she was bringing that exact quality of gentle empathy and deep warmth to bear, bringing it right up to his crumbling brink.

His breath stopped halfway. Crumbling because he couldn't not be honest with her. Fudging Uncle Carlos's role in the royal household was one thing, a scant lie, whiter than white, but he couldn't fudge Uncle Carlos back to life, pretend that a living, breathing uncle still owned this yacht. Not when, as she'd so rightly observed, there was no proof of life.

He swept up his glass, sipping to buy time. Uncle Carlos's personal possessions, and Gustav's and Hugo's, had been cleared away after the funerals. Photos and books, mementoes and magazines, jackets in cupboards. Gustav's wet-suits… A knot hitched tight in his chest. Because Gus had loved to surf, had been good at it too. Gus had been good at everything physical: climbing, skiing, soccer. Full of life. Full of energy. That had been Gustav. Always shining bright. A star. Incomparable.

'Raffiel…?'

Dulcie's eyes came back into focus, searching, gently pleading. She knew he wasn't comfortable and now him stalling like this was making her uncomfortable too. He wasn't having that, not when she was only trying to reach out, trying to be kind.

He set his glass down and met her gaze. 'I think I must look sad because I *am* sad...' Her eyes narrowed a little, urging him on. He drew in a slow breath, feeling it catch in his throat. This was going to be his first time telling someone about Uncle Carlos, finding the words himself. After the tragedy the royal aides had stepped in, handling it all, and then a few days later Papa had broadcast a statement to the nation.

Now it was just himself, the future King, addressing an audience of one, except he couldn't tell her the King part. Not yet. Too much information. For him, never mind for her. *No.* That part could wait, and everything that came with it. He drew in another slow breath, refocusing. 'My uncle died. A few months ago.'

She blinked, seemingly at a loss, and then her eyes came to his. 'I'm so sorry, Raff.' Her fingers twisted in her lap. 'Were you close...?'

He felt a hole tearing open, hot coals pouring in. Gustav... Hugo... Cousins. Playmates. Friends. *Accomplices!* He'd loved his sister, Victoria, of course, but a younger sister was no match for Gus and Hugo. Being included so thoroughly by them had meant the world. Halcyon

days. Precious times. Before their respective
paths had diverged. Before Gus and Hugo had
had to don serious suits and take a share of the
royal duties. Before he'd left Brostovenia for Cornell and a whole new life, a life of freedom and
anonymity that they must have envied. Not that
they'd ever shown it. Too noble by far for that.

*Had been...*

He felt his chest starting to buckle. No need
to go beyond Uncle Carlos, no need to tell Dulcie about Gus and Hugo, except...except maybe
it would hurt less if he shared the grief, let their
names ring out.

He swallowed, trying to shape his voice into
an even line. 'We were, yes. But the thing is...'
*Breathe.* 'It wasn't only my uncle who died. It
was...' His sinuses were suddenly burning, and
his throat, and his eyes behind his lids.

And then suddenly her hand closed over his
forearm, warm and soft. 'Who was it, Raff?'
Gentleness in her voice. 'Who else?'

Her gaze was steady, reaching in, breaking
him all to pieces, but shoring him up at the same
time, giving him strength.

'My cousins.' His voice wanted to crack but
he had to go on, make himself say their names
to honour them. He swallowed hard. 'Gus and
Hugo.'

The light drained from her face. 'I'm so, so

sorry.' Tears were mounting from her lower lids, glistening, and then suddenly she was taking her hand away, looking down, shaking her head in what looked like self-admonishment. 'I should never have asked.'

He felt a pang, a new hole tearing open, a hole with Dulcie's name on it. She'd only asked because of the sadness in him, because it was clearly moving her, concerning her, and it was concerning her because she was a kind person, warm and sweet. There wasn't nearly enough kindness in the world and here she was apologising for it. He wasn't having that.

He squeezed his eyelids shut, gathering his pain into a manageable bundle. 'It's fine that you asked, really...' Wet eyes came to his, blinking back, and suddenly the only thing that mattered was putting her mind at rest. 'Please believe me, Dulcie. I don't mind. Asking doesn't change anything. Asking doesn't make what happened worse. It can't.'

And then a fresh thought was unwinding, pulling him into a different room inside his head. Could it be that *this* was rock bottom, that going forward, even though it didn't feel like it right now, things would start to get better, feel better? Hard to imagine, and yet here he was, talking to Dulcie, feeling her empathy wrapping him up all soft and warm, feeling it lifting him. He exhaled, refocusing, feeling his perspective lengthening. 'It is what it is, and, hard as it is to accept, I can't make it not be true.'

Her eyes were moving over his face, trying to separate his pain from the bravado. And then suddenly a frown was lodging between her eyebrows. 'What *did* happen?' Her cheeks pinked a little. 'What I mean is, do you want to talk about it…?'

He bit down on his tongue. Unburdening himself to Dulcie would be cathartic but talking about the horror of Dralk wasn't an option. Brostovenia was a small country, but the freakish nature of the tragedy had created a ripple in the press. Chances were that she'd have seen or heard something, so if he were to mention Dralk then she'd know immediately who his cousins were and exactly what kind of royal 'high up' Uncle Carlos had been, and then she'd know who *he* was too.

His stomach roiled. Being untruthful wasn't his way, but what good would come of revealing everything now? It would mean dealing with, first, her incredulity and then, inevitably, the wariness and the distance that were bound to follow.

Just that morning hadn't he'd felt awkwardness hovering with Arlo, even though Arlo had known him for years? And if that could happen with a long-cherished associate, then it would happen with Dulcie too, send her fleeing, no doubt. His heart clenched. And he didn't want that. He wanted her *here*, just to *be* with her, breathing in the night air and the tang of the sea. Just breathing. Being. Being the self he knew how to be, not the one he didn't. So no, God forgive him, he couldn't tell her the whole truth. Not now. Not tonight.

He drew in a breath. 'There's not much to talk about.' *Untrue.* 'It was a car accident.' *True.* 'Gus was driving…came off the road.' *Also true.* 'The car flipped over…' *Exploded*, but he couldn't go there. He swallowed hard. 'According to the medics they died instantly.'

Which was something.

The *only* thing to hold onto.

'Oh, Raffiel…' Her voice was close to a whisper, her eyes full. 'I can't even begin to imagine…'

'I know.' He attempted a smile. 'It's heavy…'

Heavy. Sombre. And somehow not quite the evening he'd imagined, as far as he'd allowed himself to imagine anything in this uncharted landscape of randomness, randomness that had conspired to put an oblivious cyclist on a collision course with an equally oblivious Dulcie necessitating decisive action on his part, a manoeuvre that had given him an all too tantalising taste of how it felt to have her body crushed against his. Warm. Soft. Warmth pulsing through her softness in waves and that gaze, holding him, tugging at him. He hadn't wanted to let her go. And now something in her eyes was tugging at him again…

He felt sweat breaking along his hairline. Eight months lonely, eight months heartbroken. Loss on all sides, from every angle, change bearing down hard and always that endless, miserable, sapping self-pity. He was weak. Selfish. Gritless. He didn't deserve her and yet here she was somehow, fate's gift, a beautiful soul with a beautiful face, her eyes reaching in, inviting him. Definitely inviting him…

He looked at her lips, felt his pulse spiking. God, how he wanted to accept that invitation, take her beautiful mouth with his, but kissing her would lead to more and no matter how much he wanted more, no matter how much she seemed to want it too, he couldn't push that button. Dulcie didn't know his situation, probably wouldn't much like his situation, so letting things unfold would be unfair, reckless. Disrespectful! Whether he liked it or not he was going to be King of Brostovenia and until he could find it in himself to tell her that fact he wouldn't, *couldn't,* allow himself to—

'Raff…'

Husky. Urgent. *Close.* Her voice broke through

and before he could focus her lips were on his, soft and warm and perfect. He tensed, trying to resist, but then his traitorous muscles were loosening, and he was losing, folding, surrendering. He couldn't not take hold of her face, couldn't not pull her closer, taking over the kiss, tasting her, going slow, until her lips were parting, letting him into the tender heat of her mouth. And then it was deep kissing, feeling his senses skewing with every caress of their tongues, feeling desire mounting in relentless, bittersweet waves.

'Oh, God, Raff...' Hunger in her gasp, breathless need, and then suddenly she was moving, sliding onto his lap, hands winding into his hair, her body pressing closer, so close, so warm.

He cupped her buttocks, drawing her in hard until she was right there, inflicting maximum torture, throwing his pulse into overdrive, and then he took her mouth again, kissing deep, feeling her coming back at him, feeling the blood beating harder in his groin with every hot stroke of her tongue. Somewhere inside his head a pale voice was screaming, 'Stop,' but it was too faint, too distant to hear, or maybe it was just that he didn't have the will to listen.

# CHAPTER SIX

A GULL SCREECHED and her heart lurched. Just a bird, wheeling overhead. A bird! Hardly a thing to make a heart bolt but that was how jumpy she was, startling and fluttering at the slightest thing because of Raff, because soon he'd be here with that smile of his and those slate-dark eyes and those lips that fitted to hers just so.

*Raffiel...*

She felt a tug starting, transforming itself into a deep pulsing ache. She wanted more of him, all of him, had been ready to give everything last night, and would have too if he hadn't put a firm hand over hers as she'd been going for his shirt buttons...

*'Dulcie, please. Stop...' Dark eyes, dark velvet voice, ragged around the edges. 'I can't... I mean, I don't think we should...'*

*'Why? I want you. Don't you want me?'*

*'God yes! Can't you tell? But it's too soon. I think it's too soon.'*

*'Not for me.'*

*'That's just the heat of the moment talking.'*
*Slate gaze softening. 'Don't you think it'd be bet-*
*ter to wait a while?' Small head shake. 'We only*
*just met today. If we go inside now, then after-*
*wards maybe you'll wonder if you did the right*
*thing...'*

*'I don't think I'd be wondering that.'*

*Smiling. 'You have very firm opinions, Dulcie*
*Brown, but please, humour me.'*

There'd been no choice but to humour him
since he'd been putting her away from him, with
a lingering kiss admittedly, saying that he'd walk
her back to her hotel now, saying that he had to
show his face at the conference for an hour in
the morning, but that he'd like to spend the rest
of the day with her if she could manage to extri-
cate herself from Georgie and her friends.

Not a problem since she'd laid the foundations
for a Parc Güell excursion already but, even if
she hadn't, escaping would have been easy seeing as Georgie and Tilly and the others hadn't
clattered back in until dawn and were unlikely
to resurface until late afternoon at the earliest.

So now here she was perched on a low wall in
La Plaza of the World Trade Centre, waiting for
Raff, startling at the random cries of gulls, too
jittery even to have taken in much of what she
saw during her walk around the interior design

exhibition. Not like her at all. Usually she'd have been captivated, but the only thing captivating her now, *intriguing* her, was Raffiel Munoz, giddying her senses, making her act so out of character, kissing him like that...

She sighed. She wasn't in the habit of making the first move. With Tommy she had but that was different. Before then and since, she never had, in fact since Tommy she'd hardly dated. It was just that Raffiel had looked so bruised last night, so broken, that something inside had simply taken over. She'd *had* to touch him, *had* to kiss him, to take his grief and pain away, so he'd feel all the things she was feeling for him—tenderness, compassion, infinite warmth—so he'd know for certain he wasn't alone.

For a moment he'd seemed shocked but then he'd started kissing back and, oh, God, *how* he'd kissed back, taking over, taking his time, his tongue teasing and stroking hers until every cell in her body had been vibrating. And then before she knew what she was doing she'd been moving onto his lap and he'd been drawing her right in, his hands warm and sure. And then everything had started unravelling, heat and yearning taking over, and she'd felt it in him too but then all of a sudden he'd put the brakes on, delivered his speech about waiting.

She touched her lips, remembering the firm

warmth of his. That Raff wanted to wait was admirable perhaps, but it was also frustrating. She was only here for four more days, and he was only here for the conference. Not much time, not many moments to waste.

*'That's just the heat of the moment talking.'*

She felt an old chill stirring, a cold weight sinking. It was heat of the moment that had taken her over when she'd met Tommy's eye that day, wasn't it? Boldness rising up and, yes, spitefulness, offering herself to him on a plate because it had felt like a statement, a sharp kick at the world she'd come from, which wasn't a bad world, or at least no worse than any other. That was what she'd learned in the end, the hard way.

She inhaled a slow breath. Maybe Raff was right: heat of the moment couldn't be trusted. For sure it could be exhilarating, could feel momentarily powerful, but it could also lead to wrong turns, turns that kept looping on and on, dragging consequences like chains.

She looked up. Another gull was carving across the sky now, its great wings tilting. The thing about Raff, though, was that even with a few hours' thinking time on the clock she still couldn't make herself feel that getting physically closer to him would have been a mistake. They'd only just met, true, and yes, they were both only here for a short time but even so, there was something about this that felt bizarrely, sublimely right. Maybe it was that aura Raff had, that aura of strength and trustworthiness, that made him seem like a fairy-tale hero: a knight in shining armour or a noble prince!

*Noble...*

That was Raff. Saving her from the cyclist, clamping down on his own all too obvious desires when they'd been on the brink because he was thinking of *her*, imagining himself into her head, imagining next-day regrets. And it wasn't just for show, to extract consent, because she had consented, hadn't she? And still he'd held firm, walked her back to the hotel like a true gentleman. And then he'd kissed her goodnight, a long, slow, tingling kiss that had left her breathless and in no doubt that his having put the brakes on wasn't any kind of rejection. No. This wasn't about rejection, this was something else... She felt a tingle, a slow smile tugging at her lips. Could it be that Raffiel Munoz was simply an old-fashioned romantic?

She felt a fresh sigh filling her lungs. She'd grown up believing in romance, loving the idea of it, imagining how it would feel to be caught up in it, but after Charlie, all that stopped. And now here was Raffiel threatening to kindle that belief back to life, that side of herself that had always loved fairy tales and happy endings, brave knights, and valiant princes—

'Dulcie!'

Her heart bounced, then filled with a tumbling rush of happiness. Raff was coming across La Plaza towards her. Navy chinos. Burgundy and white striped shirt. Smiling, rolling his sleeves back—off duty now—his stride long and easy.

'Have you been waiting long?' His hands cupped her elbows, and then he was pulling her into his arms, warm light playing in his eyes.

He smelt nice, soapy freshness mingling with the light amber musk of his cologne. She wanted to press her lips into the hollow at the base of his throat, breathe him in, taste his skin, but this wasn't the time or the place.

She slid her arms around his neck. 'No, not out here anyway. I took a turn around the exhibition.'

His eyebrows lifted. 'And…?'

Panic rushed in. He wanted her opinion—as if it even counted for anything—but her mind was firing blanks. His fault. He was taking up all of her bandwidth with his eyes to drown in and his muscular shoulders and his cologne and his total, utter gorgeousness. *Think!* And then names were surfacing, materials and colours and shapes. Thank God! Raff might have been just a backstage minion, but it was clear that this conference meant a lot to him. The last thing she wanted was to seem lukewarm.

'I loved it. Pablo Cossa's workspace designs blew me away, and I loved Kim Goh's chairs.' He was nodding, looking pleased. 'And I really liked the emphasis on sustainability.'

The light in his eyes altered, shading towards the steely. 'It's the only way to be now. With everything. Not just architecture and design. We have to step up, take responsibility, right?'

So serious suddenly. She felt a little protective flame igniting. 'Yes, we do, but, you know, it's not all down to you personally...'

His gaze sharpened and then there was a playful glimmer coming in. 'Are you telling me off?'

The very words she used on him yesterday! She smiled inside. So they were doing this already, leaning into their own private lexicon. It felt nice, like an extra little bond gluing them together.

'No. I just think you need to cut yourself some slack, let the world take care of itself for today.'

He shrugged. 'I'm not trying to take care of the world. I'm stating the facts, that's all, adding my small voice to the chorus. We have to do better across the board, everyone knows that. It's why I—' His lips pressed together tight, and then he smiled. 'It's why the theme of the conference this year is Building Better, Living Better.'

Smiling, but not all the way to his eyes. Instead there were clouds, complications. It was getting easier to separate the different layers. Grief. Sadness. But there'd been something else too, buried in that shrug, something hiding in the far reaches of his gaze. She could always ask him about it, as she had last night, but not here. Not now.

She put a hand to his face. 'Building better *is* taking care of the world. We can discuss at length if you like, but maybe we could do it somewhere else?'

His gaze cleared. 'Did you have somewhere in mind?'

'I was thinking Parc Güell…'

His face lit, looking suddenly irresistibly boyish. 'I'm totally up for that. It's one of my all-time favourite places.'

'If your mother is half Brazilian, then that makes you one quarter Brazilian…' Dulcie was pivoting slowly, taking in the forest of columns that underpinned the Greek Theatre above them, the small scuffs of her sandals echoing slightly as she moved, and then her eyes came back to his, that irresistible little spark jumping at the edge of her gaze. 'So do you speak Portuguese?'

He felt a smile coming. 'Sim.'

'I like that.' She smiled back. 'It must be wonderful to be able to speak so many languages.'

'It's good, but it's not *so* many. I speak my native language, and English, a little Italian and I'm fluent in Portuguese, but obviously I had a head start with that one so...'

'Whatever.' She pushed her lips out, nodding a slow appreciative nod. 'It's very attractive.'

'I'm glad...' Which he was, of course. The sensual glow in Dulcie's eyes was giving him all kinds of tingles, tingles that—*admit it*—he hadn't felt under Brianne's gaze for a very long time. But talking about family felt like walking through a minefield. It wasn't that he'd minded telling her that his mother was half-Brazilian, or that Papa was heavily invested in solar technology or that his clever sister was an actuary. It was just feeling more and more wrong not to be telling her what else they were. What else *he* was. But if he told her, everything would change. All this—whatever *this* was—would disappear, and he couldn't bear that. Not yet.

A sharp pang took his heart. Of all the weeks to have met someone really worth meeting. A standout someone! Smart, creative, a little bit zany. *Funny!* Kind. Warm. Sexy as hell. Bad luck or good luck? Hard to know, hard to even think straight when she was looking at him like this. All he could think about was her lips. Tasting them. Right now.

He flicked a glance around the columned hall—

miraculously empty—then took her shoulders in his hands, walking her backwards to one of the Doric pillars. 'The question is though, Ms Brown, how attractive *is very* attractive?' Her eyes were dancing, her lips twitching, which was making it hard to keep his own face straight. 'More importantly, how can we measure its effect?'

She caught her bottom lip between her teeth, eyes twinkling, and then her hands were coming up, her fingers drawing small shapes in the air between them, parodying his own schematic in the lift. 'Attractiveness is difficult to measure empirically, but a good impression of its effect can be gained through, in the first instance, the act of kissing.'

He could feel his insides vibrating, laughter wanting to explode, but he held it in. He had to hear the rest.

She was pressing her fingertips together now, her mouth working furiously at not smiling. 'The sensations released during a kiss, sensations which might include some or all of the following—tingling, swooning, breathlessness, heart palpitations, weightlessness, and temporary loss of cognitive function—are good indicators for the effect of attractiveness. If we go to the current study, we'll call it the one quarter Brazilian study, the evidence is—'

'Stop, please...' She was too much, too funny.

Laughter was taking him, breaking him into happy pieces, and she was laughing too, a rich throatiness to it. Irresistible! He took her face into his hands. 'Did I sound that pompous in the lift?'

'No!' Her brow creased. 'You were beyond perfect.' And then her gaze softened. 'So perfect that I wanted to kiss you.'

Not just him then, in those first moments, feeling that tug.

He moved his thumbs, stroking her cheekbones, feeling his pulse quickening, anticipation tingling. 'I wanted to kiss you too.'

Her voice dipped. 'And what about now...?'

He felt his breath catching. 'What do you think?' And then he couldn't hold back, not for another second. He bent his head, brushing his lips over hers, taking her mouth, going slow. Top lip. Bottom lip. An urgent little noise vibrated low down in her throat, and then her body was rising, soft and warm, and her lips were parting, letting him into the sweet wet heat of her mouth. He felt his limbs loosening. This felt so right. So perfect. He deepened his kiss, caressing her tongue, tuning into her rhythm, feeling his pulse heating, ramping. And then her arms were going around his neck, and she was closer still, warmer still, her breasts pressing into him, her perfume winding into his nostrils.

He felt a transition taking place, his body starting to beat around his pulse. Thick, hot pulsing. Temples. Heart. Belly. Groin. He was getting hard, harder, so hard it hurt, and he was spiralling, cycling through endless opposites. He was heavy, and weightless, liquid, and solid, melting and burning. Just a kiss but the way her lips were moulding to his and that strawberry sweetness he could taste were unleashing sensations, feelings, that went beyond anything—

'Raff... Please, I need...' She was pulling away suddenly, breathless, her eyes reaching in, hazy blue, beseeching. 'I want...'

*Closer!* She wanted it and God help him, he did too, *wanted* to feel her body right up against him, like last night. He moved his hands, going for her rear, exploring its firm round contours for a tantalising moment before lifting her up, pulling her in hard. Instantly her legs wound around him, tightening, and then her hands were in his hair, her lips on his neck. Her tongue was hot, slick on his skin. He felt the faintest nip of her teeth, a gasp struggling its way up his throat. He was unravelling. Desire was King now, the only thing that mattered.

He moved them back against the pillar, felt her using its support to push against him and then her mouth was on his again and her hands were sliding down, finding him, stroking him. He felt his pulse exploding, his senses surging, spiralling out. *This* feeling… This feeling right here was the reason for not blowing this thing apart. Why on earth wouldn't he want to cling to this magic for as long as possible, drowning in her smile and her laughter, and the beautiful irresistible light in her eyes and these sublime mind-blowing kisses, no, not just kisses, *ultra*-kisses…?

'Do you *mind*?'

He froze, heart bucking, felt Dulcie freezing too. The voice was coming from behind. Male. American. Distinctly put out. There was a sense of shuffling footsteps. A multitude. *Oh, God!* Not a tour, surely. He felt his blood simultaneously draining and rushing to his face, a scalding shame curling. What was wrong with him? He was thirty-one years old. He was a king in waiting. This wasn't acceptable behaviour. What would Papa think?

*Papa!*

'Raff!' Dulcie's hiss snapped him back. Her legs were loosening around him. He moved, letting her go, catching her pointed look, a look that seemed to be saying, Don't move, don't speak. And then she was stepping around him and away, twisting her body a little one way and then the other, as if—

'That's *so* much better, thank you.' Her eyes were on his, but her voice was ringing out, clearly meant for the audience. She lifted her arms, rolling her shoulders gingerly, then with increasing gusto, and then she was rubbing her lower back, catching his eye. 'Jasper. Honest to God, you're a miracle-worker...'

*Jasper?*

Her focus shifted to the band of people whose eyes he could feel boring into his back, and then her plummy, husky, smiling voice was ringing out again. 'Listen, if anyone else here has sciatica then you totally need my friend Jasper. He's absolutely the best chiropractor in London.'

He felt his belly starting to vibrate. So he was a London chiropractor now? He wasn't going to be able to keep a straight face the way she could but he couldn't leave her to handle this by herself. She'd cast him a role, trying to save them. He had to step up, play his part. He checked in with the state of his arousal—*vanquished*—then sucked in a slow breath and turned. Immediately a dozen sets of curious, sceptical eyes pinned him. He searched the faces, homing in on a middle-aged woman whose gaze seemed to contain a grain of amusement.

He smiled at her, shrugging, digging for his inner Gustav. 'Sometimes urgent manipulation is the only way to manage an acute spasm.' He could feel Dulcie's silent mirth shaking the air

He mustn't catch her eye. One glance and he'd be finished.

He swallowed hard, shifting his gaze to a tall, stiff-faced man, clearly the one who'd barked at them. 'Apologies for how it must have looked but it *was* an emergency…' He motioned to Dulcie, taking care not to look at her. 'At least poor Jessica can walk again now. Five minutes ago she was doubled up…'

And then somehow, in spite of the situation, mischief was flaring. He shook his head, arranging his features into a frown. 'It was quite terrible to see. She was experiencing breathlessness, tingling, heart palpitations…' He slid his eyes over the faces to measure their engagement, the way he did when he was giving his conference talks. 'And all because of the—' *one quarter Brazilian effect* '—because of the pain, you see.'

'I can imagine…' This from the woman with amused eyes. She was detaching herself from the group, coming towards him with a smile. 'I suffer terribly with sciatica, myself.' Her gaze flicked to Dulcie. 'It can take you that way, out of the blue. I know.' And then her eyes came back to his. 'I'm actually in London next month, so maybe I'll look you up.' Her eyebrows flickered, amusement twitching at the corners of her mouth. 'Do you have a card?'

# CHAPTER SEVEN

'JASPER *JÚLIO*... HARLEY STREET?' Raff's voice was barely audible over the scuff of their fast-escaping feet. And then he let out a low chuckle, his eyes catching hers. 'I'm quite the bigshot, aren't I?'

'Of course! You're the best in London.'

She'd snatched the Júlio out of the air when the woman had asked for his card, because he'd seemed to be on the verge of cracking and because it had seemed like a good name for a chiropractor who was one quarter Brazilian. And, of course, Harley Street was the *only* credible address.

She smiled over. 'If you're a lie, you might as well be a big fancy one...'

Silence.

Her heart clenched. Had she really just said that, and with so much conviction? She felt her stomach hardening, a bitter taste gathering at the back of her throat. Talk about the past muscling in, twisting thoughts. Words. As if she approved of lying. Dishonesty. Was that why Raff's jaw was looking so tight? Did he think she actually believed what she was saying?

She looked away. If he did, he was wrong. Lying wasn't her way but telling big fancy lies worked, didn't it? She'd learned *that* from Charlie Prentice. Lying a big shiny lie to get her back for what she did, lying to save face, to save his miserable pride, a lie that had trapped her, changed her, but that hadn't mattered to butter-wouldn't-melt-in-his-mouth Charlie…oh, no. She bit down hard on her lip. The injustice was what had rankled the most.

Hurt.

The.

Most.

There she'd been that night after the ball, tossing and turning, trying to rationalise, trying to be fair with the blame—he'd been more than a little drunk, her dress had been a little skimpy—not wanting to say anything to her parents until she'd sorted it out in her mind, until she was absolutely certain. And meanwhile he'd been busy putting it about that in the summer house she'd confessed she was in love with him, had begged him to let her be his girlfriend, messaging his friends that he'd laughed in her face because how could she

have ever got it into her head that he'd want her
to be his actual girlfriend?

Fenced her in nicely, hadn't he, so that next
day at school everyone had been snickering behind their hands. Dulcibella Davenport-Brown
*daring* to profess love for Charlie Prentice, *deluded* enough to imagine that he'd actually be
interested. Him a senior; her a junior! On what
planet, et cetera? Never mind that he'd been the
one who'd asked *her* to the ball, the part they
seemed to have conveniently forgotten because
somehow the truth always got in the way of a
good story, didn't it?

She felt a familiar hot ache starting in her
throat and swallowed it down hard. Charlie's lie
had been bad enough, but then the whole thing
had grown arms and legs, turned personal. Not
just a junior, but a *gawky* junior, who'd looked
as if she'd raided the dress-up box for her outfit.

*'Did you see that silly puffball dress and those
shoes? Bright pink! So last year!'*

*'And what about that hair? Did you see the
state of it at the end of the evening? I mean—
hello—hasn't she ever heard of hairspray?'*

How the rumour mill had ground on, the sly
digging, the subtle bullying, but it was bullying all the same. And there'd been no come-
back because if she'd tried to put them right,
they wouldn't have listened, wouldn't have cred-

ited that the magnificent Charlie had been the one begging, begging her to let him 'do it' even as he was pinning her down, pushing sour wet kisses at her mouth, hot damp hands groping for her underwear. Standing up for herself would have meant reliving the whole thing, would have meant telling the teachers and her parents, making everything bigger, wider, deeper.

*Worse.*

She snatched a bitter breath. Maybe that was why she'd just pulled off the performance of a lifetime in the hall of columns. God, how her nerves had been jangling, but being scrutinised, all those eyes staring, weighing, and measuring, had triggered something. A fightback, no, more than that. Payback, for school, for Charlie, for all the things she hadn't been able to say to the gossips and the stirrers. A chance to tell some great big lies of her own, to protect Raff, who was looking pale and shocked.

Oh, and it had been fun, undeniably, acting a part, creating one for Raff too, wielding power over the tight-faced man who hadn't believed a word of it but couldn't bring himself to say so. None of them could. They knew what they'd seen. Unlike Charlie's friends, they'd been drawing the *right* conclusions, but what a glorious feeling, throwing a spanner in the works. Smoke, and mirrors. Roll up, roll up!

But the adrenaline was fading now, and guilt was prickling. Because what they'd been doing was wrong, not the act itself but the place, the time. They'd been out of control, behaving like kids and there was a feeling that it could come back to bite them, that any second now a hand was going to land—

She shuddered and looked back, scanning the path. No sign of the tour group, just a receding line of vacant benches, mellow light flooding in between the knobbly slanted pillars. Relief washed through, then lightness. She looked over. Maybe Raff was feeling lighter now too. The stiffness around his jaw seemed to have gone anyway. But just in case he believed that she thought lying was okay, she ought to say something, set him straight.

She slowed her pace. 'Raff, for the record, I don't actually approve of dishonesty. I was being ironic.'

'I know that.'

There was a hint of smile in his eyes, but there were also bothersome shadows. She bit back a sigh. Just when they'd been having such a good time too, flirting, and walking, and talking, him all lit up: about the conference theme, and about Gaudí, about the way Gaudí had worked with the slopes of the Parc Güell site instead of levelling it first, about the way he used mundane materi-

als to great effect. Like here, in this very promenade. Slanted rubble walls following the angle of
the hill, canted rubble pillars that somehow supported the walkway above, managing at the same
time to conjure a sense of the ancient and exotic.

But they hadn't only talked about Gaudí. She'd
prodded him about his family too—'prodded'
being the operative word since he'd seemed
strangely reluctant, but she had uncovered a half-
Brazilian mother and a consequent fluency in
Portuguese. That was the conversation that had
sparked the conflagration. Maybe going back
there would chase his shadows away.

She took a breath, slipping a tease into her
voice. 'You know, you *could* actually be a chiropractor...'

His eyebrows lifted. 'On account of what, my
extensive architectural experience...?'

Playful sarcasm. This was better.

She raised her own eyebrows back at him. *'Obviously...'*

His lips twitched and suddenly she couldn't
hold in a smile. 'No, what I *meant* is that you look
the part, and, it has to be said, *Jasper Júlio* suits
you very well. You're totally credible.'

He let out a wry laugh. 'I didn't fool anyone,
least of all the woman who's now got my made-
up number.' And then suddenly he was stopping,
catching her hands, pulling her in. *'You* on the

other hand are completely *in*credible!' Warmth in his gaze, open affection, but then his expression clouded. 'I don't know how you did that, or why really, but I feel terrible. I shouldn't have put you in that position. It was stupid. Thoughtless!' His hands tightened around hers. 'I'm so sorry, Dulcie.'

Taking all the blame. She wasn't having that.

'It's not your fault.' She pulled her hands free, took hold of his shoulders. 'It was me too.'

'But I...' Troubled eyes. 'I shouldn't have—'

'You mean, *we*...'

He pressed his lips together tight and then a narrow smile emerged. 'Okay, if you insist—*we*—but I still feel bad.'

'Well, don't. Not on my account. I *wanted* you to kiss me, *wanted* to be lifted up. I want...'

She felt her focus skewing, arrowing to the smooth swell of his shoulders, to the heat pulsing into her palms, delicious heat, like at the side of his neck, that faint salt taste of his skin before those people— Her belly clenched. How to explain, how to put words to this messy swirl of longing?

She took a breath. 'Truth is, Raff, I want to kiss you all the time, in public, in private...' She felt her hands moving involuntarily, sliding to the back of his neck. 'I want to touch you...taste you. I want to *know* you...all of you...'

A light surfaced, travelling through his gaze, and then his lips were moving, mustering what, some inexplicable obstacle? She didn't want to listen, couldn't, not when more words were rising, demanding air.

'And I know we only just met, that we're only here for a few days, but the thing is—' she could feel her skin beating, her voice trying to crack '—I can't help the way I feel when I'm with you, can't help wanting what I want, and I don't know what it means, or where this can go, or even if you want it to go anywhere but, right now, I only care about *now*.'

His lips stilled, silent.

She swallowed hard. Was she really doing this again, offering herself to a man without asking for anything in return? It could go horribly wrong, but it didn't *feel* wrong because Raffiel wasn't Tommy. Raffiel was noble, respectful, a prince among men, and this time she wasn't trying to score a point, she was just…

His eyes were holding hers, his gaze softening, pulling her in. She felt her breath leaving, her senses tangling. She was just… And then something inside was shifting, opening out, and suddenly she knew.

*I'm in love.*

She felt her heart filling, tears trying.

*Of course…*

Love was the sublime problem, and the reason for everything…her bold behaviour, impulsive actions. She was head over heels. Done for. Had been from the very first moment.

Her heart fluttered. But what to say? What to do?

She slipped herself back into the fold of his steady gaze. Still soft, still deep but shading towards the unfathomable. Was he still taking in what she'd said about wanting him, or was he reading the lines of her heart? Impossible to tell, and…impossible to tell him, because love at first sight was fairy-tale stuff, wasn't it, hardly credible? Too huge to say out loud. Oh, but if he'd only let her show him what was inside, then he'd know, feel it, and maybe she'd feel it coming back too.

Or not.

*Oh, God!* Maybe she was on a road to heartache, but how to turn back when love and desire were tingling, bright and alive, when the love part was making the desire burn harder, hotter. She wanted him more than ever, more than anything she'd ever wanted. Surely, he could see it. Surely now, after what had just happened in the hall of columns, after what she'd just told him, he'd take her back to the yacht.

Just. One. More. Little. Nudge.

'Raff…' She licked the dryness off her lips,

heart drumming. 'Do you understand what I'm saying?'

For a long second his eyes held her and then he nodded. 'Yes. You're giving me a free pass. You're saying you're happy not to think about consequences.'

But *he* had to, more than ever now, because of that confusing light in her eyes. Hazy, reaching right in, making him tingle, making his heart flip and tumble. Had his heart done this with Brianne? It didn't ring a bell. This felt new. Exhilarating. Like danger. That was what he was feeling, danger—tugging—because her fingers were playing with the hair at the back of his neck and his body was responding, hardening, and she was seeing it in him for sure, waiting for him to give in, jump on that invitation and whisk her back to the yacht.

God, how he wanted to, with every frayed fibre of his being, but he couldn't. *Mustn't!* Because no matter what came out of her mouth there was something about the light in her eyes, about her whole being, that went against the casual, something about her that commanded so much more… more respect, more care, more honesty…

He swallowed hard, willing the fire inside to die. Honesty. The biggest hurdle. The hardest. Things she had to know first, things he wanted to tell her, things he could have told her when she'd been asking about his family but hadn't, hadn't because it had felt too huge, too unwieldy.

His stomach coiled. King of Brostovenia. Twelve months away if he was lucky! He didn't want to waste precious time with Dulcie talking about it, assuming she'd even stick around long enough to listen. He wanted to enjoy her company, her laughter, that spark of mischief in her eyes. He wanted to talk about familiar things, about the things he loved, not about what was coming.

Maybe it was weak, petulant even, to be clinging to comfortable threads—Gaudí, architecture, the conference, all the passions that were burning inside—but he couldn't help it. The future was a wall he didn't have the will to breach, especially now that Dulcie was on this side of it. She was *now* and the second he told her about *next* he'd be letting next in, properly, finally. And undoubtedly it would be the wise thing, but if the wise thing scared her away then he didn't want to be wise. He wanted this, whatever *this* was, wanted to hold onto it, forget the rest…

But he couldn't forget himself, couldn't allow himself to take Dulcie to bed, do all the things he wanted to do to her until she knew the truth, because that wouldn't be right. When—*if*—they got to that stage, he didn't want to be a big fancy lie.

He swallowed hard, letting his focus drift to her mouth, her throat, that little hollow at its base where his lips wanted to go. No point trying to pretend he didn't want her, not after that spectacular public display, but he needed to give her a credible reason for not taking things further, for *rejecting* her as she was bound to see it, something rooted in truth so it would come out easily, something that wouldn't bring hurt to her eyes. Something, or someone...

*Brianne!*

The pain had been startling, real, cut the feet from under him. Why not use it, put it to work, for Dulcie's sake?

He reached up, removing her hand from the back of his neck but holding onto it so she'd know he wasn't withdrawing. 'Dulce—'

'Yes...?' Hope quickened in her eyes, then faded. 'What's wrong?'

'Nothing.' He squeezed her hand, trying to be reassuring. 'It's just that we need to talk.'

Her chin lifted. 'What about?'

'About why I'm not going to use that free pass.'

The words took a moment to register, and then her eyes were narrowing, and she was shaking her head. 'But you want me...' Her voice fell, close to a whisper. 'I know you do. Don't even think of denying it.'

'I'm not denying it.' He let go of her hand and

held both of his up high, hoping to stir a smile out of her. 'Absolutely not trying, okay.' Her expression softened a little and he seized the moment, taking hold of her shoulders. 'I'm crazy for you, Dulcie Brown. Crazy enough to have embarrassed both of us very publicly.'

She frowned. 'So why, then?'

'Because—' *how to put it?* '—you deserve a whole person and I'm not whole right now.'

'Because of your loss?'

A familiar glimmer was igniting in her eyes. Empathy. It was her go-to, wasn't it, kindness, that compulsion she had to find some fellow feeling? It made twisting truths harder, but it was for her protection and on that basis he could feel all right about it.

'Yes, but it's not only that, it's…' He looked down, rowing back, searching for the living pulse of the old pain, a pain that felt strangely distant now. But then it was coming, rising again, that ring, burning a hole in his pocket, that rooftop table booked at Gianelli's—her favourite place— that drumming of the heart, that thrill of anticipation, that getting back to the apartment, to the packed bags lined up and Brianne's cool gaze.

*It's over, Raff. We don't work any more.*

He inhaled and looked up, reconnecting with Dulcie's gaze. 'It's also that I'm still getting over someone, someone I'd planned to be with for ever.'

She blinked, her mouth folding inwards. 'You were engaged?'

'No, but I was set to propose. I had the ring, the fancy date lined up, but when I got home, she—Brianne—was packed and waiting to say goodbye.'

'That same day?' Dulcie's eyes were narrowing. She was imagining the scene, the hurt, pouring herself into the frame in that way she did.

'Yes.' He felt a pulsebeat of unexpectedly ripe bitterness. 'You could call it impeccable timing.' He let go of her shoulders so he could rub the tightness that was suddenly clamping his temples. 'I didn't see it coming. Maybe that was the problem! I was on a different wavelength.'

'Or she was.'

There it was again, that little protective edge on her voice, like in front of those poor shocked people. It was bolstering somehow, made him feel less alone.

He pulled in a breath. 'Two months later the accident happened.'

'Oh, Raff…' She was stepping in, taking his hands in hers. 'You're going through so much.' A soft light filled her gaze. 'I could help you. I want to.'

By sleeping with him, her eyes were saying. He held in a smile. She was nothing if not persistent.

'I know you do but it wouldn't be fair...' She was opening her mouth to speak but he knew what was coming, didn't need to hear it. He freed his hands and put them to her face. 'You're going to tell me you don't care about consequences, but you would because caring is what you do. It's why you're reaching out to me now, but I don't want you to get hurt, Dulcie.' He felt a tingle, a truth flying free. 'I like you far too much to risk that.'

Her eyes held him for a long moment and then she was stepping back, huffing a little stoical sigh. 'Well, that's a very sweet rejection, I must say, but, you know, it isn't a big deal. I wasn't pledging my troth or anything.' The tip of her tongue flicked over her bottom lip. 'So...' Her chin lifted. 'What should we do now?'

He felt his heart seizing. The so-called sweet rejection clearly wasn't tasting sweet. There was something busy retreating in her gaze, and the breezy tone belied the look on her face. She was paddling hard but sinking all the same, trying not to show it. *Damn!* Why was doing the right thing so difficult? Trying not to hurt her was hurting her. Trying to respect her meant rejecting her.

He felt his jaw tightening. This was all his fault. He should never have gone to sit beside her at La Sagrada Família. And yet...if he hadn't there'd have been a Dulcie-shaped hole in his life and for some reason the thought of that was unbearable.

He broke away from her gaze, looking along the promenade. Random stone bent to Gaudí's vision, made to arch, and slant. Just rubble, really, but transformed into something wondrous. That was what he had to do. Turn this rubble he'd made into something with shape, line, intent. He had to give her something, restore their momentum somehow, their lightness, but what? What did he have that wasn't heavy? *Bleak.* He directed his gaze through one of the archways. Maybe getting back out into the sunshine would help.

'I think we should walk.'

She blinked. 'Okay.'

He held out his hand. She took it, which was something at least.

He struck out, felt her falling in. This was better. Walking along, sunshine dappling through the trees, the soft warmth of her hand, the light sound of her footsteps. This was lovely, close to perfect— He bit back a sigh. Who was he trying to kid? Her hand might have been in his, but her heart wasn't in it and his was hurting. There was a silence straining, a sense of everything upending. Thank God for the fork in the path up ahead. It meant consulting. Talking.

He slowed his pace. 'Which way do you want to go?'

'I don't mind.'

Which sounded a lot like *I don't care*. This wasn't Dulcie. She'd been all lit up about the park earlier. He *had* to get her back there somehow, to that happy place, because seeing her like this was torture.

He turned to the uphill fork. 'Okay, then. I think we'll go this way…'

'It's quite steep.' She was frowning now, managing to look appealing all the same.

He felt the grain of a smile. 'Well, yes, but there's a lovely view from the top, and you like a nice a view.'

Her eyebrows drew in, puzzling.

'It's what you said on the boat…that you like a nice view.'

'Ah.' Her gaze softened. 'You remember.'

'Of course I do.' How could he forget? The slap of the waves on the hull, the warm smell of her perfume, the way she'd been leaning against the rail, smiling. He squeezed her hand. 'Barcelona at night from deck number three…' Her eyes were coming to life again, filling with a smile, filling him with hope. He motioned to the path. 'If we go up here, you'll see the whole city and the sea. I think you'll love it…'

Hair blowing against her neck. Soft black blazer, white tee, loose black jeans turned up, last night's black pumps. She seemed to like black and white, but what else did she like…? And then her fingers moved, squeezing back and suddenly his mind was clearing. *Of course…* He needed to reorientate, put her centre, not in this fretful way, in this not wanting to hurt her way, in this scared to tell the truth about himself way, but in a positive way.

'Come on.' He tugged her hand. She resisted for a blink and then she was coming, switching on her mischievous smile. His heart flew skywards and then suddenly everything seemed to be sharpening, brightening. Tangling green cascading over rough-hewn walls. Green, gold, blue whorls of flowers, clusters of white. He couldn't name them, but he was looking at them, wasn't he, properly looking, properly seeing?

He inhaled, feeling the air reaching into every part of his lungs. How the last few months had changed him, curled him inwards, set him revolving inside a loop of his own misery. But that wasn't *him*! He was no Gustav, not even close, but wasn't he known for being open, outward-looking, interested in technologies and the way things worked? He had qualities: an eye for detail, a curiosity about people and places. Brianne had used to tell him he was sensitive, and kind-hearted. Gustav had said it too, once, although he'd gone with, *'You're a soft sucker, Raff!'*

He felt a smile struggling against the sadness.

*Smiling!* That was another thing he'd been quite good at before. Because he *did* have a sense of humour. For sure, it had been lying low for a while, but hadn't it just sprung itself upon him in the hall of columns, that notion to tease Dulcie by referencing heart palpitations and so on in front of those people? That proved it! He was still inside here somewhere, all the best bits of himself that had been buried. All he had to do was dig them up.

He threw Dulcie a glance. Maybe she was feeling thwarted right now, but he could, *would*, make it up to her. He felt a smile loosening. He was going to draw her out, make her laugh, give her a lovely afternoon without taking her clothes off.

# CHAPTER EIGHT

'JUST ALONG HERE…' Raff was smiling, bouncing along with happy strides, his hand warm and tight around hers. She felt her lips curving up for the hundredth time. He was so different. Full of questions. About her studio, about life in Devon, about the landscape there. Maybe sharing his pain over Brianne had loosened him somehow. So much heartache, on top of the grief. No wonder he didn't feel whole, able to…

She bit her lip. If he'd only give her a chance, she could make him whole again, make him forget the rest, she just knew it. Her heart clenched. Or did she, actually? Was she galloping so hard along that road to heartache that she wasn't reading the signs? Warm go lights flashing then stopping, always stopping, because of Brianne, the one he'd been going to *marry*, the one he'd wanted to be his *for ever*, the one he couldn't get past, the one who was *in the way*…

She inhaled hard, steadying herself. *In the way,*

yes, but still, it was *her* hand he was holding right now, not Brianne's, and it counted for a lot that he was being honest, decent. Ironic, really. The very qualities she most admired in him were the qualities that had almost driven a wedge between them. For a desperate moment it had felt as if it was all slipping away but then he'd mentioned the view, and last night, and his eyes had been full of deep warm light, and hope had sprung up again, just like that.

Resolve too. Not to give up. Not to mess up by pushing too hard. He liked her a lot. She could feel it, and he'd said it, hadn't he? So she just needed to be patient, to enjoy this for what it was because what else was there to do when love was already living inside? If holding hands through the park was all he could offer right now, then that was fine. Romantic actually. And it *was* rather lovely being trapped inside the bright beam of his endless curiosity, seeing herself reflected in the glow of his eyes, like at this very moment.

'Here you are…' He was backstepping, pulling her from the shaded part of the path to a bright, open patch by the railing. He smiled. 'First glimpse of a very nice view.'

She forced her eyes from his and looked, felt her heart swelling. The city was below them, a hazy sweep of mostly low, tightly packed buildings. Pale gold, apricot, cream, punctuated with random clusters of deep terracotta roofs and the occasional white high-rise. Beyond the buildings under the bright blue sky stretched a bright blue ribbon of sea.

'Look…' He was motioning left, his other hand settling on the small of her back. A light touch. Warm. Like his deep velvet accent. 'Do you see it… La Sagrada Família?'

She felt a tingle, a gathering urge to slide her arms around him and pull him in for a kiss, but she pushed it down hard. No more moves, invitations. *Rejections!* Whatever happened between them now was up to him. It was for him to lead. Openly. Explicitly.

She refocused, following the line of his pointing finger and suddenly there was a different kind of tingle starting. There it was, Gaudí's basilica, its magnificent bell towers rising above the rest, a sacred place, even more sacred now because of Raff, because it was where they'd met the second time.

'Wonderful.' She looked up at him. 'It's a very nice view indeed.'

'Worth the trek?'

'Definitely.'

And then his hand fell away and he was moving to the rail, leaning his forearms on it. He seemed to consider for a moment, and then he

turned, trapping her in a warm, interested gaze.
'So, what about *your* family then…? What does
your father do?'

Her throat closed. Talking about ceramics and
improbably high Devonian hedges was easy but
talking about family wasn't. Only natural that
he was asking—after all, she'd asked him about
his family, hadn't she? But the thing was, aside
from his uncle, his family seemed like regular
people and hers were anything but.

As for herself, Raff thought she was Dulcie
Brown, a reclusively inclined ceramicist with ar-
tistic identity issues. How was she supposed to
tell him that her father was an earl, and that home
was Fendlesham Hall, a sixteenth-century War-
wickshire mansion set in eight hundred acres of
prime parkland? She might have spent the past
ten years trying to distance herself from it, but it
didn't mean that it wasn't real, or that she wasn't
part of it. Living in Devon—*hiding*—going by
Dulcie Brown didn't change who she was or what
was coming, inheriting Fendlesham and everything that went with it.

She felt a throb threatening her temples. If only
she knew how to feel about it, but she didn't.
Charlie Prentice had muddied those waters,
spoiled the taste of everything she'd ever loved,
so she'd pushed it away, but now Raff was asking and there was this panic fluttering inside

not only because she didn't want to talk about it, but because the truth was bound to throw him for a loop.

Maybe right now he was upbeat, but he wasn't in a good place generally. If he found out that she was Lady Dulcibella Davenport-Brown of Fendlesham, that she came with eight hundred acres of baggage, then he was bound to jump on the brakes again and then she'd never get herself where she wanted to be, which was up close and personal, filling him to the brim with her love so that he'd forget all about cruel Brianne.

So, no… Maybe it was wrong, *selfish*, but she couldn't tell him, not yet, which left what, lying…? She drew an uncomfortable breath. Not outright. She could never do that, but she *could* live with bending the truth a little for the sake of the greater good…

'My father is the estate manager at Fendlesham Hall.'

Raff's eyebrows ticked up.

'It's a big country house.' She slipped some droll into her voice. 'Very stately. Very English.'

'As English as pubs?'

She felt a smile unfurling. Was it really only yesterday that she'd been giving him that quick crib on England over coffee and *churros*? It seemed longer ago somehow.

'Oh, yes, probably more, actually. It's steeped

in history. There's a whole gallery of paintings.'
She stiffened her face to make him laugh. 'Grim-
faced people with big hair and doilies around
their necks.'

His eyes crinkled. 'Sounds amazing.'

'It is…' She felt a little tug inside then warmth
flooding in, mingling with nostalgia. 'It's *really*
something. Parkland with vast spreading oak
trees and tall beeches, and around the house
there's a gorgeous formal garden. I mean, *this*
is wonderful but at Fendlesham there are deep
herbaceous borders full of colour, and a walled
kitchen garden, and there's an ancient maze—
yew—very dense, a bit scary…but irresistible all
the same. I used to love riding my bike in there.'

'You got to play in the gardens?'

Her heart seized. Stupid careless tongue, running on like that. She hadn't meant to put herself in the frame and now it was too late to row
back. She swallowed carefully. Too much of a lie
to say that she'd got to play in the gardens *sometimes*. Better pressing close to the truth, then at
least she wouldn't have to be watching what she
said every second.

'I did, all the time, because we lived in.'

'Ah…' He smiled. 'I see.'

'My parents still do. Estate manager's a twenty-
four-seven job so there's no choice really. We do
have a lovely apartment…' More of a wing really

but she couldn't tell him that. It would sound excessive for an estate manager. 'To give you the full picture, Fendlesham Hall is an absolutely enormous house, a huge responsibility, a…'

'A drain,' her father was fond of saying, but always with a twinkle in his eye.

'It's open to the public six months of the year so it can be a bit of a circus. There are staff to manage, tour schedules to keep, and of course there's a gift shop and a café. My mother handles the events side.'

'Events?'

'Corporate hospitality days mostly, but we also host a classic car show once a year, and a charity garden party, oh, and we're on the books of location scouts worldwide because location fees can really boost revenue. I used to love it when the film crews came, and the movie stars…' She felt a tingle, pleasure unfurling. When was the last the time she'd enjoyed talking about home? Maybe it was the warm, interested look on Raff's face, that half-smile hovering at the corners of his mouth that was drawing it out of her, drawing all the good to the front. Like that most special memory of all…

'I remember when I was seven, Amy Madison came. She was shooting a period drama, and I was completely star struck. She was so beautiful, so elegant in her costumes that I couldn't keep away, even though my parents told me to. I'd sneak down to where the trailers were and hide, to catch a glimpse, but she always seemed to know I was there because suddenly she'd turn and beam me a great big smile. She beckoned me over one time, invited me to have tea with her in her trailer. I was beside myself, tingling all over, but she was so completely normal, you know. She just sat there in her robe, knitting, of all things, making me laugh. She was completely gorgeous.'

'I'll bet she thought you were gorgeous too.'

Her heart skipped. He really needed to stop looking at her like this if he wasn't ready to make good on the promise that was smouldering in his eyes.

She broke away, focusing on the view, but then suddenly another memory was surfacing, making a giggle come. 'I doubt it. If I remember rightly, at the time I'd just lost my two front teeth. I was all gaps. That's probably why she was always chuckling at me.'

'She sounds nice.' He was straightening, turning to lean his back against the rail. 'And your childhood sounds amazing. That's what's coming through anyway—happiness. Love for Fendlesham…'

Her heart clenched. She did love it, always had, always would. And she could have gone back, couldn't she, set up her studio in one of the outbuildings…? That was what her parents had wanted, what they'd offered her, but after Tommy it had felt too hard. She was the fallen one. Out of step, out of grace. Undeserving. And their kindness had only made her shame burn hotter, her guilt weigh heavier.

Easier to stay away. She needed breathing space, time to reflect, she'd told herself, time to *find* herself, *be* her own person. But who was she, really? Because the person she was in Devon was only one half. The other half belonged to Fendlesham. Putting the two sides back together was the thing she was struggling with.

*Putting off.*

'You haven't mentioned siblings…'

His voice pulled her back.

'That's because I don't have any.'

'Oh…' He wasn't asking but his eyebrows were lifting all the same, questioning.

'I was a difficult birth, apparently.' And she was still being difficult, wasn't she, keeping her distance, keeping to herself? She breathed through a sudden sharp ache and forced a smile out. 'My mother was advised against getting pregnant again, so that was that.'

'That's…' He seemed at a loss. 'I don't know, a bit sad…?' Warmth in his gaze, empathy. 'I mean, Fendlesham sounds like a very big place for one little girl.'

'That's true but, you know, it was a privilege too...' Such a privilege but in her mind, she'd turned it into something monstrous, hadn't she? Something to despise, because of Charlie. She pushed the thought away. 'When you think that so many kids grow up with nothing, no space inside, no space outside. I had lots of both, and I had school. Friends. And Georgie and Tilly would often come at weekends. We actually spent a lot of time together when we were kids.'

His head tilted. 'So, in spite of all your protests, you're actually quite close to Georgie...?'

'I suppose...' Her heart was thumping suddenly. How were they even talking about this? It was nice seeing interest glowing in Raff's eyes, but he seemed to be prodding all the sore spots and she didn't like the way it was hurting. And yet, maybe the hurt was a good thing. Maybe it was flagging up what mattered, what had used to, what could again if she gave it a chance, gave *herself* a chance.

She licked the dryness off her lips and then unexpectedly she felt a smile coming, tears budding. 'Georgie was always boss; always chose the game we played, but, whatever game it was, it usually involved dressing up. She loved dressing up. Still does! I haven't seen her wedding dress yet, but I know it'll be spectacular!'

'And what about you?' Raff was smiling. 'Did you like dressing up?'

He was taking in her outfit. Safe neutrals. Not pink. Puffy. *Skimpy.*

She drew in a careful breath. 'I did, yes…' Before Charlie, before all the jibing— She pressed the memory flat, forcing her thoughts past the Charlie days to the Georgie and Tilly days, and then there it was, happiness trickling back in, taking over. 'Between us, we had quite the extensive wardrobe. Georgie's best dresses came out during her ballroom-dancing phase.'

'Ballroom?'

He seemed amused—or maybe it was *bemused.*

'Yes. It's because there's a ballroom-dancing programme on the television here that's been going for years. Very popular. Professional dancers partnering celebrities. Every week one couple is eliminated…'

'Okay…'

'So anyway, when Georgie was nine, she was totally addicted, probably because of the dresses, to be honest. She learned the different waltzes and the quickstep and she taught me and Tilly, but Tilly was too short to dance with her, so that left me. We'd rehearse and rehearse, then we'd put on a show for the parents. Tilly was the presenter, and Georgie and I were the dancing couple. She was always the girl.'

Raff's eyebrows shot up. 'So you were always the boy?'

'Yes…' She felt a giggle vibrating. 'I was the ideal candidate because I had short hair back then and a suave manly appeal once my teeth grew back. Georgie would get out the face paints, give me a beard and a moustache.' She let her eyes slide over the contours of his face and felt a fresh giggle rising. 'I actually looked a bit like you.'

'Suave and manly…' He was laughing. 'I'll take that.'

And then suddenly he was folding his arms and a sweet light was coming into his eyes. 'Did you like the dancing?'

'Yes, I did…' Moving with the music, rising and falling and whirling, Georgie's face all serious, counting out the beats between tight lips. 'It was great fun, and, you know, we got to be pretty good at it. The only thing is that I'd have liked to be the one wearing the dress sometimes…'

He felt a tingle. It was in his power to give her this, the chance to waltz in a dress, to waltz as the girl. But it would mean attending the charity ball. His chest went tight. And that would mean risking the possibility of someone addressing him as 'Your Highness' in front of her.

Then again, who would actually do that? At dinner they'd be sitting with his inner circle colleagues and associates who'd known him for years and who wouldn't dream of alluding to his changed situation, or of calling him anything but Raff. As for the other guests, out of the very few who'd ever made his actual acquaintance, none of them were likely to come over because he was in mourning, wasn't he, rendered unapproachable by the grim cloak of Dralk?

If only its folds could save him from having to make that dreaded handover speech Arlo wanted. Handing over to Arlo in private had been bad enough. Infinitely worse doing it in front of two hundred people, pretending he was all right about relinquishing his conference role, but he'd endure it for Dulcie's sake... *Dulcie!* He'd told her he was a backstage minion, hadn't he? He rubbed his jaw. Still, that was a minor hiccup in comparison to the rest. He could always pass it off as acute modesty...

'You're looking very thoughtful.' She was pushing her lips out, giving him the side-eye.

His heart gave. God she was lovely and...an enigma. There was something going on with her that he wanted to get into, pull apart. The way she'd been talking about Fendlesham as if it belonged to her, those comings and goings in her eyes. Love shining out. Clouds coming in. And her voice, up one moment, wistful the next, but almost always threaded through with subtle bravado. It was something he was learning how to do too, controlling his voice, his face. It was what he'd have to do if they attended the ball, but he wasn't going to dwell on that. Far better dwelling on Dulcie, imagining her in a dress, waltzing in his arms. He felt a smile coming. It had to be worth the anxiety just to experience that. But, more importantly, this was something real, something he *could* give her and, God help him, he wanted to give it with every beat of his heart.

He unfolded his arms and pushed his hands into his pockets, going for a tease. 'That's because I'm thinking…'

She waggled her eyebrows at him. 'Funny!' And then she was pinning him with a warm gaze. 'About what?'

'About a black-tie gig I've got to attend tomorrow night…' Her eyes narrowed a little, interested. 'It's a charity ball the conference inaugurated a while back to raise money for housing projects for the homeless.'

'Sounds lovely.' Could she see where he was going with this? If so, it wasn't showing on her face. She smiled. 'And, respect! It's a really good cause.'

'It is, but here's the thing. There's dancing. Waltzing, in fact…' Her eyes lit, cottoning on now.

He felt a spark jumping, a smile twitching. 'And since you're an expert, I was wondering if you'd consider coming with me if I promise to let you wear the dress.'

# CHAPTER NINE

'YOU'VE MET SOMEONE…' Georgie's eyebrows were climbing to maximum elevation.

Dulcie felt her insides shrinking. Telling Georgie about Raffiel hadn't exactly been at the top of her to do list, but that was before he'd surprised her with his sweet invitation to the ball. Now there was no getting round it. The ball meant abandoning Georgie and the girls for a whole evening and for that she was going to need special dispensation. Also, she was going to need some help on the dress front.

She arched her eyebrows, trying to reclaim at least a little bit of the offensive. 'Could you please try not to look quite so incredulous? I do meet people sometimes.'

'I'm sure. It's just…*here*…this week?' And then Georgie's gaze sharpened. 'Is this someone the reason you left Opium early last night?'

Her insides shrank more. Georgie was too quick by half.

'Sort of.' She lowered herself onto the bed edge, trying to trim the guilt out of her voice. 'But I probably wouldn't have stayed long anyway.'

'Hmm.' And then Georgie was plonking down beside her, crossing her legs like she'd used to when they were kids. 'So spill the goss, Dulci-bella-lella. Where did you meet him?'

Her heart gave. When was the last time Georgie had called her that? And when was the last time they'd talked properly, just the two of them, leaning into their old closeness? *Georgie...* She felt a tug, warmth swelling, and then suddenly she couldn't not shuffle over, tucking her own legs up too.

'I met him here in the hotel.'

'Uh-huh…?'

She felt a tingle. 'Well, in the lift actually. And then it broke down, so we were kind of stuck—'

'Romantic!' And then Georgie's eyes narrowed a little. 'So he's a guest?'

'No. He was just visiting a business associate on this floor.'

Georgie's expression was recalibrating. So easy to read her thoughts. A man with a business associate staying in a terrace suite at the Regal was potentially the right sort. *Suitable!* But Georgie wasn't done yet.

'So does he have a name?'

'Raffiel.'

'Raffiel what…?'

Her stomach clenched. If she told Georgie that then everything would stop for a forensic examination of Raff's social media, that was if he even *did* social media! And if he did, then what if there were pictures of Brianne, selfies of him and Brianne—arm's-length smiles, faces pressed close—the girl he'd wanted to marry, the girl who'd cast him off but was still, inexplicably, in the way!

She swallowed hard. No! She couldn't let Georgie loose, raking over Raff, asking her questions she couldn't answer. Right now her heart was on the rise because of the ball, because of the way he'd kissed her when she'd said yes, as if it meant the world, as if she *were* his world. She wanted to hold that thought, keep it warm and alive. Untrammelled.

She licked her lips. 'I'm sorry, George, but I'd rather not say.'

'Why? Is he a spy or something?'

'No. He's an architect.'

Georgie's eyes clouded. It wasn't Raff's profession, it was because of *her*, because she was being secretive.

She touched Georgie's knee. 'I'm not trying to be mean. It's just that it's all so new, you know. Unexpected! I like him—a lot—and I don't want the whole thing being dissected before it's even—'

'Fine.' Georgie's lips pursed and then she flashed her palms, conceding. 'You're right, I totally would have typed his name in but it's only because I care about you.' She sighed. 'You absolutely can't get involved with another Tommy Sinclair, Dulce.'

Her chest went tight. Tommy! Still here, hanging over her even after all this time. Her fault. Because she'd never talked about him afterwards. But she could shake him off now, couldn't she, say the words to Georgie out loud?

'You don't have to worry about that. Tommy was a phase I had to go through, that's all.' Georgie's eyebrows slid up, prompting. 'He was a huge mistake, okay! See, I'm admitting it…'

'But why did you even…?' For once, Georgie's words ran out, but her eyes were reaching in, pleading.

She felt their old closeness tugging, words wanting to come, but explaining Tommy would mean tipping out the contents of the Charlie Prentice box and she couldn't do that, not for Georgie. Georgie and Tilly's school had been three counties away. They didn't know what happened at the ball, didn't know about the bullying. If she had known, Georgie would never have become friends with some of those people at uni, would never have invited them to her wedding. But Georgie had, and now *she* was going to be a bridesmaid, on parade, defenceless in front of them all over again…

Her breath slowed. Or was she looking at it the wrong way? Maybe this wedding was an opportunity to launch an offensive, a chance to look those people square in the eye and rise above them, as she had with those people in the hall of columns! She wouldn't have to say a word because they'd know, *they'd know* and maybe seeing it registering, watching them squirm, would feel like payback and she'd come away stronger. *Maybe*…

But, however she handled it, it was *her* problem. Telling Georgie would only cause an upset and, God help her, she'd caused enough upset in this family already.

She drew Georgie back into focus. 'I don't know why, George, but I've learned my lesson and I promise you: Raffiel is about as far away from Tommy as you could possibly go. He's the perfect gentleman, polite, respectful, noble, kind—'

'Good-looking?' Georgie was smiling again, mollified.

'Supremely!' She felt a tingle, a smile escaping. 'He's asked me to a charity ball at The Imperial tomorrow night.'

Instantly Georgie's face fell. 'But we're doing the sunset cocktail cruise tomorrow, remember then we're going to El Toro for tapas…'

Shame ripped through her. How could she have forgotten? The cruise had been an extra gift to Georgie from her beloved godfather, the highlight of the week. She couldn't not go, not after Georgie had been so indulgent with her, letting her off hook after hook. She felt a burn starting behind her lids, a hot ache filling her throat. When had she got so selfish, so unforgivably self-absorbed? She'd just gone right ahead, accepting Raff's invitation without even thinking about—

'Having said that, what's a cocktail cruise to a ball at The Imperial with a supremely handsome architect…?'

Her heart stopped. Was Georgie giving her this? Was that the little spark she was seeing in Georgie's eyes, the little uptick that was affecting the corners of her mouth? And then the uptick was spreading into a wide smile, and Georgie was showering her with imaginary fairy dust. 'You *shall* go to the ball, Dulcibella-lella!'

She felt a bubble of affection exploding, tears and words spilling out. 'Oh, Georgie, thank you, thank you, thank you.' She grabbed Georgie's hands, squeezing so she'd know how much it meant. 'It's going to be proper dancing, George. Waltzing!'

'What?' Georgie's face stiffened, incredulous. 'You've found a man who can waltz?'

'Yes, I have, and apparently he's something of an expert.'

'Well, in that case...' And then Georgie was drifting, disappearing into a cloud of her own thoughts, but it was easy to read them.

She held her breath, tingling. It was coming, any second now—

'You're going to need a dress, Dulce.' Georgie's eyes came to hers, warm and sparkling. 'Something fabulous!'

# CHAPTER TEN

'YOU'RE BRINGING SOMEONE…?' The surprise on Arlo's face was quickly eclipsed by a knowing chuckle. 'And is this *someone* the reason for the spring I'm suddenly seeing in your step?'

He couldn't hold in his smile. 'Probably.'

Pointless denying it. His feet did feel lighter today, his heart too, because of Dulcie, because she was coming tonight, had lit up like the Fourth of July when he'd asked her…

*'You'd let me wear the dress?' Laughing. 'Are you being polite or are you just very well brought up?'*

That line again that was theirs, that he could only answer one way.

*'Both, I hope.'*

*'Well, I'm saying yes. I'd love to go. Thank you.' Small frowning hesitation. 'I'm assuming you can dance…?'*

*'Of course.'*

*'Seriously?'*

*'Can I dance seriously, or seriously, can I dance?'*

*Fake stern look. 'The second one... Because, you know, not many people can.'*

He'd felt a sudden, unexpected stab of national pride.

*'Unless they're Brostovenian! Waltzing is a passion in my country. It's in our blood, ingrained in our culture. Everyone can dance the waltz, from folk to Viennese. We love it!'*

*Little glinting side-eye. 'And what I'm starting to love is the sound of Brostovenia...'*

He'd had to kiss her then because for some reason her warmth for his country had filled him to the brim. And it was still filling him, recharging his spirit somehow. Maybe that was what Arlo was seeing.

'So...?' Arlo's pace was slowing, his brown gaze warm and curious. 'Who is she?'

What to say? What he didn't know about Dulcie far outweighed what he did, and his curiosity about her outweighed the two put together. So much to unravel still. About that Charlie kid, for one thing, the part she'd sealed off. And there was Fendlesham too, stirring questions, and what about all her little contradictions, the deep and obvious affection she had for Georgie that didn't tally with her declaration in the lift that they had nothing in common, and those modest, monochrome clothes she wore that didn't mesh with her wistfulness about never being the one to wear the dress…

It was that irresistible wistfulness that had landed him with a speech to write and this little inquisition. Not that he minded the latter. For months all his conversations with Arlo had been painted over with gloom. It was nice having something new to talk about, even if he was short on actual detail.

'Her name is Dulcie Brown. She's a ceramicist. Very talented.'

'I'm not recognising the name.' Arlo was shaking his head. 'Is she exhibiting…?'

'No. She's here with her cousin, some extended bachelorette thing.' He felt a smile coming. 'I bumped into her at the Regal, right after our meeting, actually.'

'Wow! So now you're dating…?'

His heart pulsed. *Were* they…? They'd been on dates, sort of, but putting a label on it—

'I mean—' Arlo was leaning in, a teasing glow burning in his eyes '—are we talking about a future queen here?'

His heart stopped dead. Now *that* was a question! And yet, hadn't something like it crossed his own mind in the lift barely five minutes after he and Dulcie had met? And yesterday, when he'd asked her about her family, could he hand on heart say that his motivation had had nothing to do with trying to assess—

He swallowed hard. He couldn't think about this now, not when Arlo was busy messing with him, trying reel him in. Teasing was what they did, back and forth. Fine when it was just the two of them, but he couldn't have Arlo saying stuff like this in front of Dulcie.

He strapped on the expected smile. 'Very funny, but do me a favour, would you? When you meet Dulcie tonight, please don't mention the royalty thing.'

'She doesn't know?' Arlo's eyes narrowed into a silent, What the hell, Raff?

He felt a pang, guilt winding tight. The secrecy was gnawing at him too, increasingly, so Arlo wasn't wrong, but Arlo wasn't in his shoes either. He wasn't the one trying to hang onto bliss by his fingernails.

He offered up a shrug. 'It's a lot to lay on someone you just met.'

'I suppose…' Arlo frowned a little, and then a mischievous spark was flaring. 'And I suppose if you're just having a last little fling before—'

'No!' Anger exploded in his chest. Dulcie wasn't any kind of a fling, a girl to play with and throw away. How could his friend even go there, think that? He locked eyes with Arlo, felt his fingers curling into his palms. 'It's not like that, do you hear me? *Nothing* like that!'

Arlo's hands shot up, pushing back. 'Hey, I'm sorry. Calm down, okay. I didn't mean anything by it…'

His heart seized. Of course he didn't. Arlo was only joining obvious dots. He was here for a few days, going back to a life that wouldn't be remotely free. He'd met a girl who was also passing through, had been spending time with her but wasn't filling her in on his situation. It had all the hallmarks of a last desperate fling, didn't it?

He felt his anger draining, shame burning.

'No. *I'm* sorry. Truly.' He pressed his fingers hard into his forehead then met Arlo's gaze. 'I don't know what got into me.'

Arlo looked at him for a long scrutinising moment and then suddenly he smiled. 'Oh, my dear Raffiel, I think I do…' He lifted his chin. 'You're in love.'

'What about this fabulous pink one?' Saffy was holding the satin bodice against herself, swishing the organza skirt.

Dulcie smiled, swallowing the emphatic *No!* that was trying to explode from her mouth. Letting her revulsion hang out, all loose and flapping, wouldn't do at all. It was just a dress, and the revulsion was just a kneejerk, because of

Hemphill, and Charlie, because of the past she had to put behind her somehow, but even so, that dress… She met Saffy's hopeful gaze. 'It's adorable, but sadly pink isn't my colour.'

'Okay.' Saffy smiled a little wistfully then turned, heading back for the rails.

She felt a tug, guilt pooling. Saffy didn't need to be combing the rails, none of the girls did, because the two assistants were already hanging the prime contenders in the changing room under Georgie's watchful eye, but still, here they all were, picking things out, making suggestions. 'Dulce, this is *so* in right now…' or, 'Now, Dulce, I know it's cut away everywhere, but you've *totally* got the figure.'

How was she suddenly *Dulce* to these girls, attracting smiles and compliments? How was she sitting here like a queen bee, sipping champagne on a plush chaise longue in an appointment-only boutique on the Passeig de Gràcia, while they were all running around, helping her, *being kind*.

She felt her neck prickling. She hadn't been kind to them in her head, had she? She'd set her face against them from the start, wallowed in her own superior otherness instead of trying to get to know them. Even last night, when Georgie had announced a girls' day out, dress-shopping for Dulcie, she'd felt her toes curling while they'd all been clapping and laughing, being jolly.

She took a little sip from her glass. And they were still being jolly, weren't they, chattering and laughing? Could *she* be like that, fit in with them, being jolly? She sipped again, feeling the buzz starting. Surely, she could, after all, she had a lot to feel jolly about: Raff for one thing, his unexpected invitation, and proper dancing…

A tingle spiralled up her spine. Tonight she'd be waltzing in his arms at The Imperial, and she was going to be wearing a dress, a beautiful, fabulous *dress*! Not that she didn't like her signature style. Monochrome felt right most of the time, but it didn't address that little flamboyant corner of her soul, did it, the side that compelled her to daub colour on her wonky vessels?

She felt a frown coming. When was the last time she'd daubed colour on herself, or even worn a dress? It must have been Tilly's graduation, that black silk sheath with the high neck. Safe. Because safe was her go-to, had been ever since—

She put her glass to her lips again, letting the bubbles loose on her tongue. But safety wasn't an issue where Raff was concerned. He was safe as houses, wasn't he, the king of self-control? She felt something hard sinking, lodging inside. Because of Brianne. The invisible enemy. The one he'd wanted to marry, to be with for ever and ever and ever! She swallowed hard. Had Brianne been glamorous? Could Brianne dance?

She went for another mouthful of champagne. Maybe Brianne was a beauty, and maybe she could dance, but she was gone. Tonight it was *her* chance to show Raff a different future, to slice through those threads that were holding him. She drained her glass, not caring about daintiness. She had Georgie on her side, and, knowing Georgie, she'd have lined up a carnival of colour and flounce, some glitz and sparkle, wanting to shake poor Dulcie up, wanting poor Dulcie not to be boring. Well, that was perfect because she didn't want to be boring either. Not tonight! Tonight she wanted to dazzle, to shine, *no*, outshine everybody and everything. Tonight she wanted to knock Raffiel Munoz clean off his perch, steal his heart.

In love.

*Could it be?*

He watched Arlo disappearing through the doors of the Word Trade Centre then he turned one-eighty, striking out for Barri Gòtic. He needed some alone time, time to process the thoughts that were swarming in, like the thought that when Arlo had said what he said there'd been no spontaneous denial rearing up. Rather, there'd

been a beat of recognition, a slow steady stream
of warmth, which could mean, *might* mean—

A bright ping split the air just north of his
pocket.

He fumbled his phone out, swiped.

Having fun with the girls. I know, right? Me!
Having fun with them! Missing you, of course.
Slightly! Can't wait for tonight. D x

He felt a smile straining at his cheeks. *Dulcie!*
Of course she was having fun. How could she
not when she had so much fun inside? She was,
quite simply, funny. That stunt she'd pulled in
the hall of columns, the way she'd jumped into
the lift giggling, and what about that chuckle in
her voice when she'd declared her nine-year-old
self *suave and manly*? Not a chance! At any age.
Dulcie exuded femininity, beauty, inside and out.
She was compelling, kind, smart, mischievous,
spirited. A good person, a sweet soul. That was
why… He felt his breath slowing, his body tingling. That was why…

*I love her.*

He felt his lungs emptying, his heart filling.
Arlo was right. He was smitten! Delirious. Hope-
lessly, irrefutably in love with Dulcie Brown.

He shoved his phone back, forcing his feet
to move. Replying now was impossible. Shaky

hands, shaky heart. Epiphany happening. *In love!* It certainly explained the symptoms. *Symptoms?* Was that the right word? No other word was coming to mind, but then his mind was busy spinning, or was it his head? Both! Which meant using the crossing would be smart.

He waited for the light, then sailed over Passeig de Colom, striding up a narrow lane barely wider than his outstretched arms. Why was he stretching out his arms, not caring? Was that a symptom? *Probably.* Craziness fitted, and all the rest. The heart palpitations that came whenever she sprang to mind, which was all the time by the way, the breathlessness that took hold whenever she was near, and the hole that clanged, echoing, when she wasn't. And then of course there was the headrush that happened every time her eyes lit, the bolt to the heart that happened every time she smiled, and there was the constant craving, the longing that wouldn't leave…

He floated on, past small dim tapas bars with their chalk boards propped, past outdoor tables pressed tight against grey-gold walls, on and on through the spiderweb streets until suddenly there was brightness arriving, warmth and spangling sunshine. He blinked. Pla de la Seu. And over the square on the other side, the mesmerising Catedral de Barcelona.

He went to the wide plaza steps and sat down, trying, and failing, to steady himself.

*I love Dulcie.*

Such a feeling! New. Uncharted. Bright, alive, tingling. Miles wider, leagues deeper than anything he'd ever felt before. Was that why his wheels were on fire, why the road ahead was opening up at the speed of light, why there was not a shadow of doubt in his mind or in his heart? This love had only one future: marriage. He wanted to marry Dulcie.

His heart pulsed. But would Dulcie want him? Did she have feelings for him? He felt his wheels cooling, his heart sinking. And if she did care for him, did somehow still want him after he came clean about who he was, then would the royal aides find an estate manager's daughter an acceptable choice?

He dragged his hands down his face. Hell, if they didn't then he'd employ different aides, or he'd table parliament for a change in the law. That was in the future, the least of his problems. The biggest was explaining himself. The omissions, the half-truths.

Would she understand, forgive him?

Maybe. If she cared about him. That was his best hope: that she cared, cared enough.

He closed his eyes, conjuring the warmth in hers, that easy instant connection, that sweet tingle of fellow feeling, her touch, and the way her lips fitted to his, the way she kissed, opened for him, the taste of her...

*'I can't help the way I feel when I'm with you... can't help wanting what I want...'*

That speech, the little crack in her voice, the passion in it, her eyes reaching in, taking him all apart. He'd felt his breath leaving, hadn't he, his heart turning over? It was why he'd dug in, resisted taking her back to the yacht, because it had suddenly seemed that making love to her would be playing with her heart, the heart that was... in fact...right there... On. Her. Sleeve.

He blinked his eyes open, felt warmth flooding in. Hope. Could it be? And then his pulse was ramping because she'd said that other thing too...

*'I don't know what it means, or where this can go, or even if you want it to go anywhere.'*

A leading question, obliquely framed, one she surely wouldn't have even raised if the idea of a relationship, a continuation, wasn't already alive in her mind.

His heart plummeted. But would she still want a relationship once she knew who he was? Because in the lift she'd said that being 'on parade' was her perfect idea of hell—exact words—and yet dancing with Georgie, she'd wanted to be the one wearing the dress, the dress-up-box dress, no doubt a bright, flouncy, attention-grabbing dress! Which one was the real Dulcie?

His throat went tight. He loved them both, but it was beyond important to know, because if she *could* bear to be on parade some of the time and if she *did* care for him, then maybe the future he was already seeing could really happen, the future that, he could see now, had been coming into focus ever since she'd said that thing about starting to love the sound of his country.

A throwaway comment perhaps, but the tantalising thought that Dulcie could come to love Brostovenia had raised him up, reigniting the torch of his own pride. He could feel it glowing even now.

He lifted his gaze to the cathedral, sliding his eyes over the ornate portico. Barcelona was a fine city, but so was Nyardgat. The domed eighteenth-century palace, the parliament building with its grand neo-classical façade, the soaring gothic cathedral. Modernist galleries and museums, the old quarter with its narrow streets and jostling half-timbered buildings.

He felt a smile coming. Nyardgat was a crazy, paradoxical city and Brostovenia was a crazy, paradoxical country. Yes, there was poverty and there were religious divisions, but what country in the world didn't suffer those? And what country in the world didn't elect disappointing governments from time to time? But there were elections coming, new faces emerging, full of passion and promise. And there was a new king coming too, wasn't there…?

He braced himself for the drop, for the shrinking feeling to start, but there was nothing, just the glow burning inside, a kinetic thrum building. He touched his forehead. No tension. No ache behind the eyes. No grey fog.

He leaned forward, resting his forearms on his thighs. Clarity was good. Logic!

No, he wasn't Gustav. He wasn't handsome, or daring, or charming in that easy, boyish way of Gus's, but that was all right, because he had other qualities. Experience of the wider world, of living in other countries as an ordinary person able to do ordinary things. Laundry, taking out his own trash, buying groceries… He knew how it felt to have a bag split, provisions crashing onto the sidewalk in a liquid splatter, knew how it felt to miss the last train. He understood the small everyday challenges of the ordinary world, which *had* to be a desirable trait in a monarch. And he understood business, more than understood it. He was good at it! Success in the States. Success in Paris. *Awards!* Earned through hard work, not by leaning on his royal connections.

Could he use his passions and experience to good effect when he was King, force improvements in the country, be more than a face and a title? He felt his pulse quickening. For one thing Brostovenia was too reliant on coal and the government wasn't doing enough to change that. Green energy was the only way forward. Everyone knew that. He could spearhead the campaign, push hard, be a thorn in the side, a pain in the ass. He felt a tingle, a smile tugging. Hell, if the state thought that King Raffiel Munoz was going to keep his mouth shut and his nose out of politics, then they were very much mistaken!

He blinked. And here was the Raffiel he recognised! Alive, questing, starting to imagine the challenge, not just imagining it, but relishing it. This was more like him. Papa would recognise him now. He'd be smiling, thinking, *That's* my son.

*Papa...* He felt his chest constricting. Poor Papa. Dealing with everything, looking for support from *him*, for strength, strength he hadn't been able to find, but it was coming back now, running through his veins. He was going to step up, take the weight off Papa's shoulders. He was going to make everything right, make Papa proud.

He shook himself. But first, and most importantly, he had to tell Dulcie everything—*tonight*—face up to what he'd done. His heart stumbled. But telling her before the ball might ruin everything. She might not come, and he couldn't risk that. He'd promised her a dance and if a waltz turned out to be the only thing he could give her, the only thing they'd both have left, then it had to happen.

Which meant, telling her afterwards. Straight after.

He got to his feet, pressed his hands to his face. That way, if she didn't like what she was hearing, at least he'd be able to see her back to the hotel, know that she was safe. His heart clenched. At least there'd be that.

## CHAPTER ELEVEN

So PINK, THEN, after all. Not bright, and not remotely puffball, but still pink...or rather, ashes
of roses.

*'Like a vintage rose...'*

That had been Georgie in the fitting room,
looking all pleased with herself.

*'I bet you thought I was going to put you in
red with diamanté, didn't you?'*

*'Well...'* It was what she'd been hoping for.
Something bright. Dazzling. The opposite of
monochrome but definitely *not* pink.

*Little frown. 'Red with diamanté is me, dar-
ling, but you're softer, more romantic. Old rose
suits you, and the drape is divine. Twirl for me...'*

She'd twirled dutifully, liking the feel of the
lifting silk, liking the appreciative little noises
Georgie was making.

*'That handkerchief hem is going to flare even
more when you're dancing, and mid-calf's perfect.
It isn't swamping you.'* And then Georgie's hand

had shot out, stopping her mid-pivot. *'As for this low back...'* Mischievous gleam. *'You'll be able to feel his hand, every little movement.'*

*'Georgie!'*

*'Georgie what? It's what you want to feel, isn't it? I mean, you're clearly besotted—'*

*'Am I?'*

She'd felt peeled back suddenly, involuntarily defensive, but Georgie wasn't having any of it.

*'Er...hello? You're all glowy. Dreamy-looking. The last time you looked like this was when you were in love with Amy Madison. I'm just putting two and two together...'*

And then Georgie had pulled her round so they were face to face.

*'Look, I get that you're not ready to share, but it's obvious you've got the deep feels for this Raffiel fellow. And I don't know if he deserves them or not, but for now I'm on your side and, trust me, so is this dress! Elegant. Romantic. Quietly but seriously sexy. It's you, Dulce! One hundred per cent. Honestly, he's going to die when he sees you.'*

Not quite the result she was after, but still, it was a lovely dress, and if Georgie thought it was perfect, then that was endorsement enough.

She reconnected with her reflection, feeling the little seismic shock all over again. It *was* herself looking back, but also not. Impeccable make-

p, courtesy of Saffy, a few fine braids plaited
nto her hair—Tilly's gleeful idea—all of it swept
p into a Boho chignon by Georgie, and—she
moothed her hands over the bodice—this beau-
iful dress.

She touched the straps. Wide. Silky-soft. Such
n unexpected day. Getting to know the girls,
aughing with them, making them laugh, feel-
ng included. Properly included! They had their
n jokes, yes. And, yes, they did love Ascot and
Ienley, but they loved other things too. Saffy
ad just run a charity half-marathon—'Ran it
ike a tortoise, darling!' And Peter's eldest sis-
er, Katherine, was learning how to sign because
not enough people can'.

Bottom line: the girls were nice. Lovely! And
hey were her friends now, seemingly, excited
or her date with 'the waltzing architect', blow-
ng her air kisses, throwing her little over-the-
houlder winks as they'd filed out, heading off
or their sunset cruise.

'If you don't come back tonight, we'll know
ou where you are…'

Her heart dipped. Would she be back tonight?
he didn't want to be. She wanted to be on Raff's
acht, being unwrapped by him, loving him all
ight long, but there was Brianne, wasn't there?
Reining him in for some inexplicable reason,
he ex who was supposed to have been his for

ever but who'd thought nothing of leaving him just like that. No discussion. No trying to work things out!

How could she have done that, walked out on someone like Raff? More to the point, how could he still be getting over her when she'd treated him that way? It didn't make sense, and it definitely didn't fit with the fond light in his eyes, or with his toe-tingling kisses. Oh, and what about the way he'd kissed her after she'd said yes to the ball? That had been a whole new level of warm and deep, achingly tender, as if he'd been trying to fill every one of her senses up with himself. No reticence. No taste of hurt in his mouth. No trace of Brianne in *that* kiss!

She picked up her clutch, turning it over in her hands. What to make of it, of him? Holding back, not wanting to hurt her, but also not holding back, asking her to the ball, kissing her senseless, with *crazy for you* vibes coming off him in great big waves. It was there in his kiss, in his gaze, in his touch, and if she was feeling it then surely it had to be real, and if it *was* real, then why—?

A sudden bright knock swept the thought away.

*Raff!* Stubbornly insistent about coming up even though she'd said she could meet him in the lobby. Stubborn. Noble.

*Here!*

She drew a quick breath and hurried through the suite, noticing the unfamiliar tap of her heels on the terrazzo, the tremble threatening her knees. Just thinking about him standing on the other side of the door was giving her delicious shivers. Black-tie Raff… He was bound to be the hottest black-tie guy she'd ever seen because there was no one like him. No one. Her belly quivered. Question was, what was he going to think of this new pink Dulcie?

'Hello, Raff!'

'Dulce! You're—' He felt his lungs emptying, his senses scrambling. Where to look when every detail was heartbreakingly perfect? Face, dress, hair. Milky skin, those straps that, by the way, looked as if they'd push off her smooth shoulders without too much encouragement, and that bodice, the pleasing swell of her breasts.

His pulse jumped. He'd felt her breasts pressing into his chest every time they'd kissed, felt his hands straining at the cuffs he'd shackled himself with, wanting to touch, desperate to. But he couldn't go there, couldn't let himself think about what he wanted to unfold, what might happen, or not, depending on how things went later. Hard enough tamping down the rogue thought that she looked every inch a queen: elegant, beautiful, radiant.

'You're stunning, Dulce.'

Doubt, of all things, ghosting through her gaze. How could she not know how perfect she looked when she was incomparable?

'I mean it.' He loaded his voice, so she'd feel how much. 'You're exquisite…'

The words were registering now, drawing her smile out.

'Thank you.' And then her head was tilting with the tiniest frown. 'So are you…'

Was she seeing it? Any second now, surely… She was looking right at him after all. He felt a chuckle agitating under his ribs and dropped his gaze, adjusting his cuff to hide his smile. 'Thanks, but a suit's a suit.'

'Not when it's bespoke, which yours obviously is. You look very…' Small silence. 'Very…' Long silence.

He felt the chuckle agitating more. Surely, she was seeing it now…?

He looked up to check. Still frowning. Unbelievable! She was able to spot a bespoke suit—black, boring—but the most obvious thing of all—*the most obvious thing*—seemed to be eluding her. He couldn't wait. The gift in his pocket was burning a hole. Also, the car was waiting.

'Dulcie.' He jerked his thumbs towards his face. 'I shaved.'

'Oh, my God!' Her hand flew to her mouth.

'That's it! I can't believe I didn't see it straight away. I was thinking you looked brighter some-how, younger—'

'I'll take brighter and younger...' And vital, and happy; all the things he felt around her.

And then suddenly her hand was coming to his cheek, flattening against it all warm and soft. 'So, what did the beard do to deserve its un-timely end?'

He felt his breath catching, a sublime but un-welcome heat stirring. 'Nothing, other than that it didn't belong.'

Her eyebrows ticked up.

She wanted him to expand, meanwhile what he wanted was to put his hand over hers, bring it to his lips, then pull her close, kiss the place where that little loose tendril was touching the side of her neck. But he couldn't. Mustn't. Be-cause if he did then they'd never get to the ball. Poor Arlo would be left scratching his head, Dul-cie wouldn't get her dance, but, most importantly, he'd be breaking the promise he'd made to him-self not to make love to her until she knew who he was. *What* he was. His stomach clenched. A conversation for later. Right now there was this one to finish, and then the gift...

'The beard was an aberration.' He felt the grief inside shifting and stretching, trying to storm the air in his lungs. He swallowed hard. 'I let a lot of things slide after—'

'Of course.' Cutting in so he didn't have to say the words out loud, caressing his cheek to soothe. She was so tuned in, so quick to stretch her imagination in his direction. And then she was removing her hand, stepping back, her gaze gentle. 'Do you want to come in?'

And talk about it, was what she was really asking, wanting to pull him into her fold, tuck kindness around him. A beautiful trait. One of so very many. Not that he actually needed kindness. Fact was, in spite of the momentary dip, he was fine. The beard might have grown out of misery, but shaving had been a joy. Cathartic. Seeing his features emerging. That feeling of: Here I am after all, better, stronger. *Ready!*

He drew her back into focus. But he *did* need to go in so he could give her his gift. It was why he'd come up, after all.

He smiled. 'That'd be good, just for a minute.'

The suite was similar to Arlo's. Same lofty sitting-dining-kitchen space, same full-length windows running along. The view was of darkness now, peppered with a scattering of distant lights: buoys, boats, a plane winking its descent.

'I know how it feels, Raff...'

Her voice spun him around.

'...walls caving in, soul shrinking, that heaviness inside that makes doing even the smallest things impossible…' She was setting her purse down, coming over, her eyes glistening at the edges. 'I know all about it because of Charlie, or rather, because of what happened afterwards…'

His ribs went tight. The car was waiting, and his gift, but he couldn't interrupt. This was the bit she'd snipped off before and now, to make him feel better, she was going to share it, even though it was costing her. He felt his heart contracting. She was trusting him with something she'd never spoken about to anyone before.

Trusting *him*.

He caught her hand, folding it into his. 'What did happen?'

Her gaze drifted then came back. 'After Charlie did what he did I didn't do anything or say anything for the reasons I told you before, but Charlie did.' Her lips pressed together. 'He told everyone that I'd declared undying love for him, that he found it hysterical.'

'Making you the butt of a joke to save his bruised balls and ego?' He felt his gorge rising. 'How fricking mean! How pathetic!'

Her eyes registered acknowledgement. 'And effective. Putting me down made it impossible for me to climb back up. Anything I said to counter, you know, like *the truth*, would have sounded like I was trying to get back at him because he'd spurned me and not the other way round.' And then, unbelievably, she was shrugging. 'Nauseating as it was, I could have coped, but unfortunately at my fine, upstanding school *pathetic* grew arms and legs…'

Her eyes closed for a long moment. When they opened again, they were gleaming wet, tearing at his heart. 'In no time at all I went from sad, lovelorn junior to sad dresser, sad student, all-round sad individual. Sad Dulcie. Droopy Dulcie.' A tear was rolling down. He went to catch it, but she stopped his hand. 'Please, it's fine. I just need to finish.'

Hurting but strong as well, determined. He felt admiration flaring, anger burning a hole in his chest.

'It affected me so badly that after exams I couldn't bear to go back. I persuaded Mummy and Daddy to let me go to sixth form college. Fresh start and all that, but even then, I couldn't raise myself back up. Not for the longest time.' And then her gaze sharpened into his. 'You couldn't bring yourself to shave. I couldn't be bothered to wash my hair. I'd just throw on a black beanie.' Her eyebrows flickered. 'Black became my go-to. Black everything because it didn't require an ounce of thought, a single ounce of effort.' She took a little breath. 'So that's how I know what it feels like to lose yourself, and I wanted you to know that, to know that if you want to, you can talk to me…'

Dry-eyed now. Calm. Killing him, making his heart hurt. *Bullying!* That was what she'd endured. Keeping it all to herself, working through it alone because she hadn't wanted to upset her parents, their friendship with Charlie's parents, putting herself last, thinking, what, that everyone else was more important?

He reached for her other hand, so he had both of hers, so he could squeeze love into them. 'I wish you didn't know it, Dulce; wish you hadn't had to go through that.'

'The point is, I *did* go through it, and guess what? I'm still here, still standing.' She smiled, and then she was stepping back, tugging his arms full stretch, twisting, swirling her dress, powdering the air with her perfume. 'You could even say I'm in the pink…'

Those eyes, reaching in, so full of warmth, so full of… He felt hope tingling and pushed it down hard. One thing at once.

'You certainly are, pink, and lovely…' He felt a smile stirring. 'And too far away.' He pulled on her hands.

She stilled, her eyes sparkling. 'Too far away or what?'

He felt his smile breaking, spreading. 'Come here and I'll show you.' He pulled again and then she was coming, letting him tow her in until she was right there.

She cocked an eyebrow. 'You weren't thinking of spoiling my lipstick, were you?'

He'd been thinking about the gift, but now he was totally thinking about her mouth! Dewy. Lush. That sweet strawberry heat inside it. He swallowed hard. But he couldn't go there, couldn't risk letting himself loose inside her kiss.

'I'm thinking about it, but there's a car waiting and also—' he let her go, slid his hand into his pocket '—I've got something to give you.'

She faltered, eyes widening. 'A present?'

'Yes...' His fingers connected with the velvet case. Would she like what was inside it, or would she think it was too much? His heart creased. As if anything could ever be too much for Dulcie. That was the thought that had overtaken him in the Pla de la Seu, the thought that had sent him on a three-hour quest through the city looking for the perfect piece, something she'd love, something to signal at least a portion of what he was feeling if she turned her back on him before he got to declaring it. A cold river ran down his spine. Would she do that?

He drew out the box. No point thinking about it now, not when her eyes were quickening, shining. He licked the dryness off his lips. Maybe downplaying his efforts would be wise though, just in case she hated it.

He sprang the lid, heart thumping. 'It was a whim, okay, but I hope you like it...'

Baroque pearls, multiple strands of them glowing on twisted silver link chains, different lengths, some fine, some bold and chunky. An asymmetrical piece, edgy, Boho, and absolutely one hundred per cent her kind of thing.

She felt her heart giving, her breath struggling to come. 'Oh, Raff...' She looked up, catching a flicker of needless anxiety in his eyes, eyes that seemed so much larger and darker now that he was clean-shaven, gorgeously, smoothly handsome. 'What can I say? It's beautiful. I love it.'

A smile broke his face apart, relief shining through, and then he was lifting the necklace up, making it clack and tinkle. 'It's platinum.'

Her mouth went dry.

'I thought you'd prefer it to gold because you seem to favour silver.'

Silver, yes, but platinum was in a different league. Rare. Precious. *Expensive.*

She felt her pulse stumbling. What was she supposed to make of a gift like this? What to think? *How* to think even when his gaze was tight on hers, warm, deep, making her heart drum and drum. Was this Raff holding himself back? Because pearls set in platinum didn't say holding back. The question was, what were they saying? He'd called it a whim, but it was obvious he'd chosen it with care, matching it to what he knew about her, what she—

'So, you like it…?' He was looking anxious again. 'Really? You're not just saying it?'

She felt tenderness blooming, tears prickling. How could he be so insecure when he'd chosen the most perfect gift imaginable?

'No, I'm not just saying it.' She put a hand to his face. 'I love it.'

*And I love you.*

Could he see it in her, feel it pulsing through her palm, all the things she wasn't saying? Maybe she ought to tell him, but then again, wouldn't that be hijacking this sweet moment, the moment he'd designed for her, held close to his chest while she'd been rambling on about her downward spiral, letting it out—*admit it*—as much for herself as for him, because she'd *wanted* to share, felt safe enough to?

She ran her eyes over his face. Open. Kind. No guile hiding in his corners. That was the thing about Raff. He was safety. Sanctuary. Talking to him was so easy because he was good, strong, anchored in all the right places. That was how she felt. But he'd said he wasn't strong, that he wasn't whole. Where was he, emotionally, right at this moment? Was losing the beard a sign that he was finding his feet, a sign that Brianne was fading from view?

Her heart dipped. And what about the necklace? Was that a sign too? Was she closer than she knew, winning? Her heart dipped again. Oh, God! If Raff was emerging from his sadness, coming back into himself, then she *had* to tell him the truth about herself. Only…maybe not now because the car was waiting, wasn't it, had been for a while? She inhaled a slow breath. Later, then.

Soon.

She blinked him back into focus, felt warmth surging through her veins. What mattered right now was showing him her delight, every scrap of the love she was feeling inside.

'I really *do* love it, Raff. Thank you.'

'I'm pleased.' His eyes held her, a deep considering look, and then he was undoing the clasp, smiling. 'Shall we see if it fits?'

# CHAPTER TWELVE

'RAFFIEL TELLS ME you're a ceramicist…'

Arlo was sliding into Raff's empty seat, setting his wine glass down.

Kind brown eyes, warmth in his smile, so why were her nerves suddenly chiming, and why was her tongue thickening, sticking fast? She'd felt calm and confident earlier, walking in on Raff's arm, appropriate, pretty, happy. Happy to stop and smile for the conference photographer—laughing, actually, because of Raff crooning nonsense into her ear the whole time.

'Chin up, darling…that's it…work it now…more…that's it…fabulous!'

As for the venue: perfect ballroom, perfect royal-blue walls and gleaming parquet, perfect glittering chandeliers and tables dressed in white linen, laid with silver and crystal, candles glowing in tall candelabras. And the dinner had been perfect too, every morsel delicious, not that she'd managed much. Too busy staring at Raff, drink-

ing him in, the easy way he had of talking to the
people at their table, not just Arlo, who was his
friend, but the others too. No trace of that inner
sadness, just smiling eyes and keen interest in
whatever it was they were saying.

Raff had stayed close, kept everything rolling along, made her feel as if she belonged, but
now he was gone—*where?*—and it was like
being back at school again, feeling eyes she
couldn't bring herself to meet burning her skin.
She touched Raff's necklace. His eyes had been
burning too when she'd turned round to show
him how it looked but she liked that burn, the
way it melted her in all the right places. It didn't
sting like this.

She swallowed. Maybe the trick was to copy
Raff, simply show the face she wanted everyone
to see, like at Parc Güell. She'd pulled the wool
there all right, hadn't she? And probably it was
just her imagination anyway, dragging her back
into the old dark tunnels, imagining slights, vi-
cious whispers. *Silly!* Because these people were
grown-ups, not stupid teenagers with petty agen-
das. The glances she'd caught earlier had been
admiring, so why would they be different now?
She *was* dressed to the nines, and she *was* with
the hottest guy in the room, even if right now he
was mysteriously absent, so if she was feeling the
heat of curious eyes then no wonder. She needed

to pull herself together and get on with it. Also, she needed to reply to Arlo.

She drew him back into focus, smiled. 'That's right.'

'You haven't thought about exhibiting here?'

'Erm…no.' It was impossible not to laugh. 'I'm afraid I'm a long way away from being international calibre.'

Arlo raised disbelieving eyebrows. 'Raffiel says you're very talented, and believe me, when it comes to art and design, he knows what he's talking about, so if you change your mind, you could submit for next year…'

She felt a little tingle. So Raff had talked about her work to Arlo Ferranti, praising it. Rating it. Wonky vessels that for her always fell short, that didn't quite express the wonkiness inside, or whatever intangible thing it was that kept her at it, battling, questing, trying to pin herself down—

'Raffiel's such a powerhouse.' Arlo was talking on, his eyes alive with obvious affection. 'He has so many interests. Passions! And of course, he wants all of them represented, so he's grown the conference year on year, so now it's this behemoth…'

She felt a frown coming. 'What do you mean, *he's* grown it?'

Arlo picked up his glass. 'Well, when he started it—'

'*He* started it?'

'Yes.' Arlo's eyebrows twitched up. 'Didn't he say?'

'No.' She felt a hollow beat thumping.

'Ah…' For a piece of a second, he looked uncomfortable, and then he smiled, shaking his head indulgently. 'Well, that's Raff all over. Mr Modesty.' He took a sip from his glass. 'What did he tell you, let me guess, that he straightens the tables, puts out the chairs…?'

*I'm one of the many backstage minions.'*

'Something like that.'

Arlo laughed and set down his glass. 'Well, the truth is, it's his gig.' And then his expression altered, clouding a little. 'When he put the first one together it was here.' His eyes lifted, circling the room. 'Can you imagine?'

Right now it was hard to even think straight. Why on earth hadn't Raff told her that it was *his* conference, *his* baby? Modesty was one thing, but it didn't make sense, unless for some unfathomable reason he'd thought she wouldn't be interested…

'I mean, this space is a fair size, but when you consider how big it's got…' His eyes came back to hers. 'Raff moved us to the World Trade Centre three years ago so he could add an interior design exhibition, a partner event to offset the tedious—' he comedy slapped his head '—oops! Did I really say that? I mean the *fascinating* debate about the future direction of architecture and—buzzword alert!—sustainability.' A smile filled his cheeks. 'In case you haven't noticed, Raff is passionate about sustainability...'

Just yesterday, that fire in his eyes at the World Trade Centre:

*'We have to step up, take responsibility, right?'*

And she'd said it wasn't all on him, said he should cut himself some slack and he'd got a bit defensive then, hadn't he, told her he wasn't trying to save the world...? Her heart clenched. Had she inadvertently offended him? Surely not, because he'd been fine afterwards, excited for Parc Güell. She bit her lips together.

But who knew what was really going on inside him? Easy imagining that she *knew* him because she could *feel* him, because of the connection that felt real, because of the love that was exploding inside, but the truth was, she didn't know Raff at all. How could she? They were barely three days old. How could she know all the things that made him tick? The only thing she knew for sure was that she wanted to. More than ever now.

She lifted her glass, shooting Arlo a smile. 'I think I might have picked up on that.'

Arlo's lips pressed into a knowing grin and

then his focus suddenly shifted to a point beyond her left shoulder. He flashed his eyebrows in that direction and then he was pushing his chair back. 'If you'll excuse me, I'm being summoned...'

'Of course.' She felt panic fluttering. First Raff and now Arlo! What was with all the disappearing? She swallowed hard, painted on a smile. 'Erm...before you go, do you know where Raff is?'

'Yes.' He nodded to the same spot behind her. 'He's over there.' And then he split a grin. 'He's the one doing the summoning.'

Dulcie was twisting round, looking over, her chin tilting up in that quizzical way she had. He shot her a smile then looked down at the mic in his hand, riding out the swell of faint guilt. Maybe it had been a poor decision not to tell her about the speech, but mentioning it in the limo would only have spoiled the joy of sitting beside her, breathing in her perfume, drinking in her excitement, her astonishing beauty.

And it would have led to questions, opened doors into rooms he couldn't enter yet. But when he'd been writing it—short and sweet because who wanted to listen to him droning on when the stage belonged to Arlo now?—it had seemed like an opportunity to lay a few bricks, drop some hints, to prime her. That was the thinking, anyway, thinking that had felt sound at the time.

'Hey!' Arlo was arriving, beaming warmth. 'I like your Dulcie very much. *È molto carina, proprio bella.*'

Raff glanced at Dulcie again, felt his heart filling. She was still looking over, one slender arm draped over the back of the chair, a small smile playing over her lips. She most certainly was a beauty, and so much more.

He met Arlo's gaze. 'Tell me something I don't know.'

Arlo leaned in. 'So what are you going to do about *you know what*?'

The truth, Arlo meant.

He felt a knot pulling tight. 'I'm going to tell her tonight. After we leave.'

Arlo's gaze faltered, then the light inside it intensified. 'It'll be fine. You'll see. The way she looks at you... I mean, you've got to be feeling it, Raff.'

He could, the warmth pouring out of her, making his heart sing, but whether it was love or just—

'It looks like the real thing, my friend.' Arlo was smiling. 'That's what I'm seeing anyway, and the real thing doesn't care about royalty. You're still you at the end of the day, whatever it says on the label, and it's *you* she's crazy for.

Arlo, *Italian*, the eternal romantic.

Could *he* believe it though? He wanted to, but how were things really going to play out? In this place, right now, he was a free man, but that was about to change and it wasn't as if he and Dulcie had had time to establish roots. The root-growing part was still to come, that was, if she was even interested in trying, because dating him wouldn't be easy.

Spontaneity was out for a start. And outside the confines of the palace and the various other crown properties in Brostovenia and Switzerland he was always going to have a security detail at his shoulder. Discreet perhaps but nevertheless there. And in the public eye, in the public mind, dating translated as *courting*. Fine by him, because that was his intention anyway, but for Dulcie it could feel like ridiculous pressure, and if things didn't work out, then she'd be trailing him behind her everywhere she went. *The Prince's ex*.

It was a lot to ask of anyone, never mind someone he'd only just met, someone whose life was determinedly insular, someone who was looking at him right now with a sweet, perplexed gaze. The knot inside pulled tighter. *Dulcibella.* She didn't know it, but it was thanks to her that he was turning himself around. She'd lit his candle, kindled him back to life, given him a view that went beyond the bars of his cage.

And now it was starting, the process of opening up the view for her in return.

*Baby steps.*

He looked at Arlo. 'Are you ready?'

Arlo grimaced. 'As I'll ever be.'

'Right then.' He switched on the mic, tapping it to quieten the room, and then he drew in a breath. 'Good evening, ladies and gentleman…'

'So you were never *just* a minion…?' Dulcie was frowning a little, a glimmer of hurt behind her gaze. 'Why didn't you tell me?'

'Because…' Getting into the intricacies would have been sailing too close to the royal patronage thing and he hadn't wanted to get into all that with her on day one. God help him, he'd just wanted to be Raff Munoz, the lift guy, the guy she'd liked well enough to have coffee with. But *baby steps…*

He drew in a breath. 'Because it didn't seem that important given that I'm stepping down—'

'Because of new challenges.' Her mouth tightened a little. 'New horizons.'

Quoting his own speech back at him. He hadn't been specific. The people closest to him knew where he was bound. The rest didn't care. They were here for charity, for a good night out or, being cynical, they were here to be seen doing the right thing for charity, to be snapped at the doors in their finery. It didn't matter. They'd paid handsomely for their tickets, pledged further donations as well as extravagant auction prizes for next year. The money, every cent of it, would go to building villages for the homeless, providing them with support services to help them get their lives back on track. That's what mattered, and that the charity ball was now an annual fixture in Barcelona. Year after year, the money would keep rolling in, and if, from the lofty heights of the Brostovenian throne, he could keep pushing for—

'Are you at least going to tell me about your new challenges?'

Dulcie's clear blue gaze came back into focus, reaching in, pleading almost.

His lungs locked. God, she was lovely, and he hadn't even kissed her yet, had barely dared to touch her. Too scared at the hotel in case he'd unravelled but somehow they'd got here intact, were still intact. Pristine in fact.

*Enough!* His speech was delivered. The crown was Arlo's now, the responsibility, the work. Meanwhile the orchestra was striking up, and the girl he loved was looking at him, her gaze softening, registering the music, the changing vibe in the room.

He felt his heart dipping then lifting again, a smile coming. 'I'm going to tell you all about it later, I promise, but right now I want to dance with you...'

Warm light filled her eyes, warming him right back.

He pushed up out of his seat, holding out his hand. 'Will you do me the honour?'

'You know I will...' She was laughing now, taking his hand, rising. 'It's what I came for.'

# CHAPTER THIRTEEN

So MAYBE RAFF hadn't filled her in about his exact conference role but right now it was impossible to care because she was in his arms, being whirled around the floor, and his dark eyes were locked on hers, full of warm, brimming light. Such a feeling, dancing under sparkling chandeliers, dress swirling exactly as Georgie had said it would. She felt a smile curving. Georgie would *so* love to be in *these* pink silk shoes, dipping and gliding with such an exquisite partner, feeling these warm fingers at her back, moving, caressing…

Her breath hitched. There they went again, shooting electric tingles along her spine, and here he was, pulling her closer, leaning in.

'Have I told you how much I like this dress?'

She breathed him in, savouring his deep, musky warmth. 'Only about a hundred times.'

'Apologies for the repetition.' His fingers moved

lower, a lingering stroke, bolder. 'But I just can't stop thinking it.'

Thinking *it*, and what else? Because if his talking hands were telling the truth, and the dark glow in his eyes was real, then his mind was on the same track as hers. And yet, he hadn't so much as kissed her. He'd given her an exquisite, thoughtful gift, but no kiss. Not in the suite, nor in the limo.

She felt her heart sinking. Was it Brianne, still—in spite of the gift—wielding her invisible strings? How could that even be possible when every nuance of his body language was sending tremors through *her*, making *her* pulse drum? How could a part of him still be possessed by Brianne when she was feeling his possessiveness flowing around *her*, feeling it in the firmness of his hold, in his unswerving gaze? And what about that gaze…? So adoring. So tender. Tender for *her*. Adoring *her*.

Crinkling. Smiling. Leaning in.

'You dance beautifully, Dulcie.'

She felt a blush tingling. 'Right back at you.'

He laughed, then spun her hard, and suddenly she was laughing too. She could feel her heart soaring, all her doubts vaporising. Raff was filling her to the brim, to the tips of her senses. She was so high she didn't even know if there were any other dancers on the floor. All she could see was his handsome face, all she could feel was...

*Everything.*

But what was the use of feeling everything if she couldn't give it, make him feel it? Her heart clenched. In three days she was leaving. Would she be leaving empty-handed? Was she going to be forced to rebrand whatever this was as her 'little Barcelona fling'? How could she do that when it was less than a fling but felt like more?

She tore her eyes away from his, fixing on the impeccable bow at his throat. In a million years she couldn't have foreseen this, imagined that this could happen to her. A hen week in Barcelona and now, somehow, she was head over heels with this man, this extraordinary man who was confusing her every which way. Saying he was crazy for her but holding himself back out of, what, respect? Uncertainty? Her heart clenched. She was tired of aching and wanting, tired of not being able to do anything about it because she'd resolved not to push him, determined that it was for him to take the lead...

But then, actually, what was he doing now if *not* taking the lead? His fingers were sliding under the silk cowl at the base of her back, stroking circles, stirring that ache. She felt a tug, her focus skewing. Oh, God, his touch was sublime, assured, definitely *not* ballroom, and definitely *not* ambiguous. This was her signal, the very one she'd been waiting for! He was making moves on her, as far as was possible mid-waltz, and what was she doing? Not signalling back was what, just staring dumbly at his tie.

*Stupid, Dulcie!*

She swallowed the smile that was rising and lifted her eyes, sliding her hand from his biceps to the back of his neck, nice and slow so he'd know she was reading him down to the small print. 'By the way, have I told you how hot you look in this suit?'

'Hot?' He seemed surprised, a little abashed. 'I thought I looked fitting. Smart.'

She felt her heart melting. Did he really have no sense of how imposing a figure he cut, no sense of how handsome he was, how sexy? It was endearing, made him even more attractive.

'Well, you *do* look smart, of course...' She stroked his nape, circling her fingers, smiling inside as a satisfying little glitch interrupted his gaze. 'But also, you *are* hot. If we were to unbutton this—' she gave his collar a tug, enjoying the sudden flare of his nostrils that betrayed his sharp intake of breath '—loosen the tie, you'd graduate to full-blown smoking hot.'

His chin dipped. 'If you unbuttoned me, people would notice.'

Three days left... Nothing to lose.

She loaded her gaze with every iota of in

tent she possessed. 'Not if we were somewhere private...'

His lips parted, moving silently, and then suddenly she was being pulled in tight against him, his voice in her ear torn black velvet. 'Do you have any idea what you're doing to me?'

The raw emotion in it stopped her breath. He was holding her so close now that it was verging on the indecent, but he didn't seem to care. He was waltzing on, turning her deftly, every powerful movement of his thighs making her weak, giddy. She could feel wetness gathering between her legs, the ache inside building and building.

She turned her head to catch his eye and her belly clenched. He was burning up with it too, openly, feeling the same hurtling desire, the tantalising crush of their bodies, the heat, and the swirl, feeling the ache of the music, the flow of silk, the soft rub of wool, the warmth in the room, the scorch of their skin, his fingers, her back, her fingers, that damp softness at his nape, and then the tempo was slowing, and the music was ending.

Ended.

For a heart-thumping moment his eyes held her fast, and then he leaned in, lips grazing her ear. 'Let's go.'

'Wait...'

Her heart lurched. *Wait?*

He was pulling away, raising himself onto his elbows, his hair falling forwards over his forehead. 'I need to tell you something…'

She felt her cells screaming. He couldn't be doing this, not now that they were actually alone in his stateroom, not after that blistering kiss in the lobby of The Imperial, that wild, hungry kiss that the concierge had interrupted none too politely with a loud, disapproving cough; not after asking the driver to raise the privacy screen in the car so they could keep kissing all the way back, kissing and touching, hands sliding… Raff's hand sliding under her skirt, driving her pulse into the red zone.

All this foreplay, days of it, it felt like, and now they were tumbled on his miles-wide bed, blissfully private with the lights down low, and his tie was hanging loose, those top buttons finally undone, and he was beyond super-smoking hot and now—*now!*—he was putting the brakes on!

'Can't it wait?' She could hear the whimpering frustration in her own voice. 'I mean, it isn't that I'm not interested…' She put a hand to his cheek, catching the soft ripple in his gaze. 'But I don't want to talk, Raff, not now. I just…' She looked at his lips, imagining where they could go, and suddenly there was a flood crashing through, breaking her voice to pieces. 'I just want what I want. All of you.'

His gaze held her, burning, and then the burn mellowed to a deep, soft glow. 'You can have all of me, Dulcibella, everything…' And then he smiled. 'Just not all at once.' His smile became a chuckle. 'If you'd had your way, we'd have been naked on the back seat of the limo.'

She felt a smile twitching. 'Are you telling me off?'

'No.' The corner of his mouth ticked up, acknowledging the familiar line, and then he was leaning in, brushing his lips over hers. 'But I need to tell you that I'm not in a hurry, and you shouldn't be either.' His mouth came to hers again, warm, brief, teasing. 'I want to slow things down, give you the attention you deserve…'

Those eyes…that velvet voice…full of promise. She felt her insides melting and aching at the same time.

'Come…' He was sitting up, pulling her up too.

Electricity arced up her spine. He was in control now. It was there in the confident set of his shoulders, in his darkening eyes. She felt a delicious weakness threading through her veins. He'd demonstrated his physical strength in the hall of columns, in the easy way he'd lifted her up, and she'd felt it in him while they were dancing too, but this was a different kind of power, a different side of him, a side that was making her senses sit up, making her blood quiver.

He leaned in. Another kiss. Slow, sensuous, electrifying and then his fingers went to the loose lock of hair that was tickling her cheek. He tucked it behind her ear. 'I love your hair like this...' His eyes came to hers, crinkling. 'Little plaits.'

Her insides went limp. Surely on no planet whatsoever had 'little plaits' ever sounded so sensual.

'My cousin Tilly's idea.'

'She has good ideas...' His focus drifted to her hair again. 'But I want your hair loose now.' His eyes snapped back. 'Is that all right?'

'Of course...' Anything for him, especially when his gaze was taking her apart like this.

She reached up to take out the pins but immediately his hands were on hers.

'No. Let me.' He was smiling a hazy smile. 'I want to do it.' He released her, shifting back a little. 'Turn round.'

She turned, feeling the nakedness of her own back, the weight of his eyes and then it was his hand she was feeling, on her shoulder, and his lips on her neck, trailing kisses into her nape. She felt her nipples hardening, hot darts arrowing to her core.

How could he stand to string things out like this? He'd been rock-hard on the yacht, rock-hard at Parc Güell, and rock-hard in the limo. His body had to have been on fire but still he was putting her first, taking his time for her. *Loving her.*

She felt tears welling behind her lids, the love inside surging, and then it was his breath she was feeling, and warm lips behind her ear, and his left fingers unclasping her necklace. It clacked softly as he set it down, and then his fingers were back, tracing a warm path up her spine to her shoulders. She closed her eyes, leaning into the tingle, the quiver, the ache of his touch.

And then his hands were moving over her head, searching for pins, pulling them out with excess gentleness. She felt section after section falling down, his unhurried fingers combing through it.

'I'm not going to attempt the plaits…' She felt his smiling breath in her hair, the press of his shirt against her back, insane heat punching through it, and then his hands were on her shoulders again, sliding her straps off. She lifted her arms free, felt the silk bodice falling into her lap.

A burning silence. Just her heart drumming and then that voice.

'Look at me, Dulcie.'

Her core tightened and pulsed, wetness soaking into her underwear. How could an accent do that, stroke her in places that fingers couldn't reach?

She licked her lips and turned.

His breath caught audibly and then his eyes were sliding down. She felt her nipples hardening more, craving his fingers, his mouth, his tongue and then suddenly he was moving, easing her backwards, fire in his eyes, and something else that triggered a heart skip.

'God, you're beautiful...'

Hands in her hair, lips scorching hers, and then he was moving down, trailing kisses along her collarbone, nipping and sucking, lower and lower, his breath warm on her skin, and then his hands were sliding over her breasts, caressing, his fingers teasing her nipples until the sharp pulsing darts were firing in volleys. She arched her back, wanting his mouth, and he was right there, reading her need. For an instant the wet caress of his tongue felt like balm, but then the low-down yearning was back, stronger than ever, relentless, overpowering...

'Raff, please...' It came out cracked and dry, but it was all she could do to get it out at all.

'What do you want, baby?' His head lifted. 'Tell me what you want...'

Her pulse spiked. That accent, those words, smoky eyes burning into hers. Dishevelled Raff. Suddenly her favourite ever view. How to tell him she wanted everything he was, all of him, not just this, but how could she tell him that when

he didn't even know who she was? She'd planned
to tell him, and maybe she could have in the
car, but the moment they'd got in he'd asked the
driver to raise the screen, and his eyes had been
full and deep, still burning with the dance and
that lobby kiss and she simply hadn't been able
to stop herself from sliding onto his lap—

'Dulce…' His lips grazed her nipple again,
sending a fresh spike pulsing through and then he
was shifting himself back up, his eyes searching,
his gaze deep and full. 'What do you want…?'

Those eyes, blue as the ocean. No wonder he
was drowning…

So much for noble intentions. Could a dress
be held to account? Because Dulcie in *that* dress
had been his undoing. He simply hadn't been able
to stop his fingers from caressing her skin while
they were dancing, hadn't been able to resist sliding them lower and lower, and then the wheels
had been coming off, and all the wheels within
the wheels. Impossible not to pull her close, to
feel that close wasn't nearly close enough. Like
in the hall of columns, fever taking over…

Close dancing, *ultra-dancing*, blood pumping, the slightness and lightness of her, her hands
in his hair, and her smooth skin, and the warm
floral pulse of her perfume. When the music

stopped there'd been no logic operating, no saying the things he needed to say, only desperate hunger for the softness of her mouth, that strawberry heat inside it, and then the concierge had coughed, and the lobby he hadn't even noticed walking into had snapped into focus, people going by remarking with their eyebrows, and all he'd been able to think then was that he *needed* to be alone with her, to tell her who he was before the fire consumed them both.

And then it was getting into the car, asking the driver to put the screen up, barely drawing breath before Dulcie was on his lap, kissing him, pulling at his tie, pulling him to pieces, shredding his resolve. She felt so right in his hands, so right in his heart, and God help him he'd tried to tell her, but she'd overturned him, slayed him with her open desire, that fatal crack in her voice. And now he was all split open, ready to be her slave and he wanted to hear it from her lips, what she wanted him to do.

He drew her back into focus, felt his pulse ramping. He knew what *he* wanted. He wanted to tear off the rest of that dress, explore every inch of her skin, make her whimper, moan, climax with his name on her lips, and then he wanted to sink himself inside her, bring her to ecstasy again, and himself. God, how much he wanted that sweet release, an end to this torment of hard

pulsing desire that had been his basic state from
the moment she'd opened her hotel door. But he
needed to hear it, needed—

'I want *you*, Raff…' Her gaze was deep, full,
making the love inside surge and froth, and then
there was playfulness surfacing, that little spark
at the edge of her gaze. 'I want you on your back
first and then, after that, I want you every which
way, all night long, so please—' she wriggled
sideways '—roll over.'

He rolled, obeying, liking the gleam in her
eye, the way the light from the bedside lamp was
bathing her firm little breasts. She rose up onto
her knees, pushing the dress over her hips. Pale
underwear came into view, tiny, see-through. He
swallowed hard. A smile touched her lips, and
then she was coming for him, straddling him,
going for his last three shirt buttons, lifting the
fabric away.

Silence.

'And there I was thinking you couldn't look
any better.' Her eyes came to his, a tiny, perplex-
ing glisten in their corners and then her hands
were moving over his skin, caressing, stroking,
fingers running warm tingling trails, lower and
lower.

He felt his breath coming in patches, his eyes
wanting to close. His hardness was insistent,
throbbing, and definitely not lost on her because

she was moving back, undoing his button, unzipping him. He felt a gasp arriving, hissing through his teeth. *Sweet heaven*, she was all over him, fingers moving, thumb sliding over his tip, teasing him, shuffling backwards. He felt his fingers curling into his palms, anticipation beating. He was desperate for her to do what she was setting herself up to do, but…no… *No!* What he wanted more was to be the one in control, to go down, then go inside. He wanted to watch her face, kiss her mouth, feel every beat of her heart, her heart beating close to his. *That* was making love…

'Dulce…' He rolled up, so they were face to face. 'I don't want you to do that.'

She blinked. 'Ever?'

*Ever?*

His heart pulsed. Did 'ever' mean that she *was* thinking beyond Barcelona, thinking that there could be other nights, days, weeks, beyond this one? A relationship…? He felt his heart speeding up. That glisten in her eyes before, that extra layer hovering in her gaze, the magical, compelling, irresistible layer. *Was* it love…for *him*? She wasn't saying it, but he was feeling… Oh, God, and he wasn't saying it either, was he? Because when he declared it, it had to come from the lips of Prince Raffiel Munoz, not Raff Munoz, architect. His heart creased. But he couldn't tell her now, not when her eyes were taking him apart like this, not when all the love inside was pleading for release.

He put his hands to her face. 'No, I'm not saying *ever*...'

A slow smile curved on her lips. 'Good.'

# CHAPTER FOURTEEN

A LOW, insistent buzzing noise filtered in, then grainy light, then the sound of gentle breathing. She turned her head. *Raff!* Sprawled on his front, sleeping, his features soft, his lips slightly parted, his hair a sort of dark nest. She felt a smile tugging. Her fault! His hair was longer than it looked when it was combed back, too irresistibly soft not to touch, to bury her fingers into at critical moments.

She suppressed a giggle. So many critical moments. A whole night of them! A whole night of loving, of feeling loved, of feeling her own love pouring out, wanting to say it but not saying it because first she had to tell him who she was, so that the truth could be true from every angle. Her chest went tight. Would he be upset that she'd lied not twenty minutes after telling him that she didn't approve of dishonesty...and what about her title? Would that bother him? It didn't seem likely somehow, not after seeing him in action at the conference, the way he could talk to people, the confident way he'd delivered his speech. He'd fit right in at Fendlesham, that was for sure. Better than she did.

She felt a frown coming. There it was again, that weird buzzing—

*Phone!*

On the low drawer unit by the door.

Bound to be Georgie, checking up, wanting all the luscious details. As if she'd even go there! As if she even could. The words hadn't been invented yet to describe how she was feeling inside, what she was feeling for Raff, but she couldn't leave the phone buzzing. It was going to wake him, and after the glorious, toe-tingling night he'd given her, Raffiel deserved to sleep!

She slipped out of bed, snatched up his shirt from the floor then tiptoed out.

Ten missed calls from Georgie!

*Ten!*

Her heart slipped sideways. Had something terrible happened…an accident…someone hurt? She forced her feet along the corridor, heart pounding, pulling on the shirt, fumbling with the buttons. *Oh, God!* Tilly's nut allergy! The sunset cruise people had been informed but that didn't mean—

She slammed through the door that led to the upper decks, taking the steps two at a time until she was on the third. At the rail, she drew in a deep breath, and tapped dial. The thing was to sound calm and reassuring. If Tilly was in the Emergency Room, then Georgie needed her to be—

'Dul—cee—bella—lella…'

She felt her heart righting itself. What was that law about the simplest explanation being the most likely…?

'Morning, Georgie.' Trying to lure Georgie away from her teasing wouldn't work but trying was reflexive. 'How was the cruise?'

'It's almost afternoon, sweetie. And the cruise was delightful. Meanwhile, what *I* want to know is exactly *when* you were going to tell me about Raffiel.'

'I sent you a text…' From Raff's hot lap in the limo, admittedly, so there might well have been typos, but still, the scramble of words should have made sense.

'I'm not talking about that.'

'What, then?'

'God, Dulce, this is *me* you're talking to! Please, don't be disingenuous.'

*Disingenuous?*

She felt a vague flutter of panic. 'I'm not; I don't know what you're getting at.'

'Really?' Georgie's voice was dripping with a sort of affectionate sarcasm. 'So there's nothing *massive* you want to tell me about the waltz-ing architect, no extra tiny thing about him that a cousin might have wanted to know first-hand instead of discovering it on social media—*trend-ing*, by the way—along with some interesting pictures and a frenzy of speculation?'

Her chest went tight. *Pictures? Speculation? Trending!* She felt a queasy sensation lodging in her stomach, old ghosts stirring, grey shades of school morphing into full colour.

'Georgie, please. I don't know what you're talking about...'

Silence.

'You *are* joking, right?' Georgie's tone was darkening, making the jumping panic inside jump higher.

'No...'

'So you're telling me you don't know that Raf-fiel is a prince...'

*Prince?* For a beat the word came into focus, solidifying, and then quickly it was turning to liquid, vaporising. Georgie was pulling her leg, winding her up because she hadn't gone back last night. Raff wasn't a prince! He was an architect. A regular person, moving through the world in a regular way, doing regular things... If he was a prince, he'd have an entourage. A bodyguard! If he was a prince, he would have told—

'You're deafening me with your silence, Dulce…'

'Oh, I'm sorry.' She felt a smile tugging. 'That must be just the sound of me not falling for it.'

'I'm serious, Dulcie. Your Raffiel is Prince Raffiel Munoz of Brostovenia!'

Her heart clutched. She hadn't told Georgie Raff's surname, or where he came from—

'And soon he'll be the King of Brostovenia because of that horrific accident at Dralk racing circuit…'

*Prince… King… Dralk…*

Dots were dancing, peppering her vision.

'It was all over social media a few months back, and there was a big spread in *Hello!* magazine as well because Prince Gustav was a bit of a celebrity, being a handsome prince *and a* racing driver.'

*Racing driver?*

'It was awful. He spun out on the track, flipped his car over into the royal stand. The explosion killed him and the King and his younger brother. Surely you saw it…?'

Words tumbled.

Surely…surely…surely…?

*No!* She hadn't seen it because she didn't look at social media, didn't follow the news. And now she couldn't even breathe but Georgie wouldn't stop talking—

'Raffiel's father is King just now, but his health isn't good, so it's expected that Raffiel is going to be taking the throne within the year. That's why the pictures of you and him are going viral. You're hashtag royal romance. Also, it doesn't hurt that the two of you look beautiful together...'

*Beautiful...?*

Her throat closed. There was nothing beautiful here. Raff was a liar! Not noble, not gentlemanly but secretive, conniving. *Cruel!* How could he *not* have told her who he was? How could he have sat blithely listening to her pouring out all her pain over Charlie, listening to how Charlie had taken her in, pretending to be the golden boy, pretending to be courteous, and decent, and responsible, when the whole time *he* was doing the exact same thing? How the hell could he have sat there *pretending* to be moved, acting all concerned when he was hiding behind a great big lie?

'Dulcie...' Georgie's voice came in like an echo bouncing. 'You mean to say that Raffiel hasn't told you any of this?'

'No.' The word crept out, tearing a hole. Saying it out loud, admitting it out loud hurt so much. Her ignorance. Her stupid gullibility. She felt wetness scalding, seeping, the hot messy clog of it in her lashes, the thick ache of it swelling in her throat. She couldn't talk, couldn't bear to, not here. She squeezed her lids shut, swallowing hard. 'George, I can't do this now, I'm sorry.' She killed the call. Powered off.

What kind of fool was she? Falling for the wrong man a*gain*, falling for lies. Sad Dulcie. Droopy Dulcie. *Stupid Dulcie!*

'Dulcie!'

Her heart pulsed. And now he was here, faltering at the top of the steps, his face taut. From the look of him, he'd just got the news too. He seemed to gather himself, and then he was moving, coming over.

She felt her stomach hardening. So what was he about now, coming to lie to her a bit more, break her heart a little bit more?

He stopped a pace away, his eyes reaching in. 'I'm so sorry, Dulce…'

That voice, shredded velvet. Those stricken eyes, tugging at her even now, even when he was the cause, even though he'd lied, even though because of him she was now *trending* on social media, a prime target for a bit of shooting practice, sniping. Pulling her to pieces, pulling pieces right off when all she'd done was fall in love. She felt a sudden searing stab of anger. She'd never got the chance to tell Charlie Prentice his fortune, but she sure as hell was going to tell Raff his.

She lifted her chin. 'Is this what you call a *royal* apology?' He blinked, recoiling a little. 'When were you going to tell me, Raff, or maybe you weren't going to bother?' She offered up a shrug. 'It's a minor detail after all.'

His mouth tightened visibly, a sudden flash of steel at the edge of his gaze. 'Well, *Lady* Dulcibella *Davenport*-Brown, if we're talking about minor details…'

Her heart seized, then burst into angry flames. 'Don't you dare do that! What I did doesn't even come close to what you did. I *told* you about Fendlesham, that I lived there. The only thing I didn't tell you was that it belongs to my family.' His mouth was opening, forming a *'why'* but she wasn't finished—not nearly.

'I told you about Charlie, how he pretended to be nice—decent—and you didn't think to tell me then, didn't *think* to yourself that pretending to be a normal person when you're actually a prince would be a *huge* deal to me; didn't *think* that, after all the nastiness I went through at school, the possibility of being photographed with you—quite likely in view of your being a *prince* and everything—being splashed all over social media for even more people to laugh at would be a fricking *huge* deal…' And then a fresh thought was pulsing, ripening in her mouth. 'Or maybe you don't care. Maybe your head's so full of Brianne that you can't see beyond—'

'Dulcie, stop!' This was insane. Last night he'd poured himself into her, body, and soul, and now she was dredging up Brianne! 'This has got *nothing* to do with Brianne.'

Her lips clamped shut, but her eyes were still blazing, wild hurt pulsing behind them, tearing his heart out. He needed to dowse this quickly, then explain. Try to.

'I was going to tell you everything after the ball last night.'

Her chin lifted. 'Easy to say now.'

*For the love of God!*

'I'm not just saying it. It's why I asked the driver to raise the privacy screen, but then you were all over me, didn't give me a chance…'

Her eyes registered the truth of it, and then her chin was lifting again, defiant. 'Raff, you're six foot two if you're an inch, and I'm…' she frowned '…much smaller. You could have stopped me!'

'Maybe but…' Hands under his shirt, her lips scorching, tongue snagging, drawing heat through, sending heat pulsing… He felt a tight breath leaving, caught a flicker of acknowledgement travelling through her gaze.

'I tried again when we were downstairs—'

She blinked, and then the mask she was wearing slipped, relenting a little. 'I remember, and I didn't want to hear it, but, Raff, it wasn't exactly a choice moment.' Her lips tightened again. 'The choice moment would have been day one. You could have told me then.'

'Could I?' His heart pulsed and then suddenly torrent was rising, pushing up all the pain and bitterness. 'What if I couldn't find the words? What if it seemed too big to talk about, too damn hard?'

She blinked again, and then suddenly there was that familiar gentleness filtering in. He felt a tentative seed of hope germinating.

'Dulce, I haven't been straight with you about who I'm going to be, and, God help me, I'm not trying to defend that, but I've been completely straight with you about who I am, because *this* is me.'

Her gaze opened into his more, warming him, inviting his hand to reach for hers, making his heart leap when she didn't pull away.

'I'm an architect, spent seven years training to become one, loving every second because I live and breathe architecture, and art, and design. It's why I founded the conference here in Barcelona, because Papa brought me here when I was fourteen to inspire me, to show me Gaudí's work. *This* is where it all started for me and...' His heart clenched. 'And it's where it all ends too, not because *I* want it to, but because Gustav—'

He swallowed hard, trying to push it all down, so he could keep speaking, explaining, so she'd understand, so she wouldn't hate him. 'For months I've been stacked high with grief...

anger…bitterness and… I just didn't want to get into that with you. I didn't want to talk about what was coming because I don't know what's coming. My whole life, I've been free, Dulce. I carved out a niche, doing the thing I love, and now I'm next in line, where *next* means *soon*, because Papa isn't strong, and I don't know how to be what I have to be now, but I have no choice.'

Her eyes were full, glistening, which had to mean she understood. Would she forgive him though?

He squeezed her hand, loading his gaze. 'Thing is, I never expected you to come along, but you did. I was moping because I'd just handed *my* conference over to Arlo, and you jumped into that lift laughing, and you seemed like sunshine to me. I was praying that the lift wouldn't get fixed, but when it started moving I realised that, because of who I am, asking you out was impossible, so I forced myself to walk away.'

'Oh, Raff.' Her eyes were soft on his, glistening more.

'But then there you were again at the basilica, and it felt like, I don't know, fate or something. I couldn't not come over, but I didn't have a plan, or any expectations. I simply wanted to *be* with you, bathing in your sunshine. I told myself that as long as I didn't let things go too far, as long as I didn't hurt you, then it would be okay.'

Her gaze slipped for a beat. 'That explains why that first night you wouldn't—'

'It isn't that I didn't want to.'

'I kind of got that at Parc Güell…'

'Not my finest hour.'

'And Brianne was what…?' Her eyebrows flickered towards a frown. 'An excuse…?'

'A plausible reason, in lieu of the real one…'

Her eyes clouded. 'But you could have told me then, surely…?'

'What, and have you look at me differently, treat me differently?'

'I wouldn't have…'

'But I didn't want to take that risk because you seemed to like Raffiel the architect, the normal guy. I was scared that if I told you the truth then you'd disappear on me, and I didn't want that to happen.'

'But if you'd told me, then I'd never have had to…' she faltered, and then her eyes came back to his, glistening all over again '…then I'd never have had to lie to you about who I was.'

'You thought it would bother me?'

Weariness in his gaze. Gentleness.

'I don't know.' She felt her thoughts jostling, pushing, and pulling. 'You'd just been telling me about Brianne, about how you didn't feel like a whole person, and I panicked. I thought my title would intimidate you…'

A smile touched his lips. 'It doesn't.'

Of course not. He was a prince. She was a Lady. It was almost poetic. So why wasn't there relief tingling, a sweet lightening sensation happening?

'Dulce…?' His eyes clouded and then his fingers tightened around hers. 'What's wrong?'

'I'm just…' She felt her words fading. Last night, he *had* been going to tell her who he was. Undeniably. At the dance, promising to tell her later about the new *challenges* he'd mentioned in his speech, and there'd been that urgent edge on his voice when he'd asked the driver to raise the privacy screen, urgency she'd interpreted as… and then he'd pulled away from her in the state room, trying again. *And* he'd given her the necklace, chosen with obvious care. Pearls.

*Platinum!*

After all the sidestepping, last night he'd been set on telling her the truth, but why? Why then?

She drew him back into focus. Concern in his gaze, but behind it, something burning, something that had been burning all night long, something she'd felt in his touch, in the way he'd made love to her. *Oh, God!* She felt a sob wanting to rise. Was Raffiel in love with her? Was that why he'd suddenly felt compelled to tell her the truth?

She felt her heart twisting out of its socket. It was what she'd wanted, wasn't it? Because she was in love with *him*, had been from the first moment, but now he was somehow a prince, a prince who was soon going to be a king, a king who was going to need someone confident and poised by his side, sure of who she was, and maybe that was where he was going with all this, where this was all leading, but she wasn't confident and poised, was she? She was a girl with a title she couldn't use, hiding in Devon, making her wonky vessels, stamping *Dulcie Brown* on the bases because she was too scared to be Lady Dulcibella, to take the good and bad that came with it.

Her heart seized. And that was the truth right there, the real reason why she hadn't told Raff who she was. Maybe five per cent not wanting to spook him, but a hefty ninety-five per cent because Fendlesham wasn't all tea with Amy Madison and playing dress up with Georgie and Tilly. It was whispering at school and burning cheeks. Having. To. Endure. And it was weaponising Tommy. Causing. Pain. It was Pandora's box, a stuck genie festering in the bottle, impossible to open, impossible to talk about.

'Dulce...?' His hands were suddenly on her shoulders, his gaze deep and full. 'Look, I know it's been a hell of a day so far, but we're still here, aren't we, still standing? And maybe this isn't the

best time, but I want to know…' He swallowed.
'I *need* to know if you can see—'

'*Camisa bonica, Senyoreta Dulcibella!*'

Raff flinched just as her own heart jumped.
And then there were more voices, and a rattling
whirr of camera shutters from the quayside,
flashes blinding her, and Raff's strong arm going
around her, her feet barely touching the deck as
he bundled her inside.

'Are you okay?' He was breathing hard, searching her face, fury dancing behind his gaze. Protectiveness. That whole irresistible noble thing
he had going on.

And then her heart was buckling, hurting.
He'd been about to ask her if she could see a future for them. It had been there in his eyes, the
hope unwinding, but how would it be, dating
him, continuing? Would it be like this, lenses
aimed all the time, taking her apart, even on a
private yacht?

*Yes…*

Because it happened all the time, celebrities
caught unawares for the gossip mags. And now
she was 'it' for the second time in twenty-four
hours, on the way to going viral in nothing but
Raff's dress shirt, and, just like with Charlie, she
couldn't hit back, couldn't *do* anything, except…
Her heart pulsed. She *could* go home. Not to
Devon—no security there—but to Fendlesham.

The family wing was private. Private garden. Nice high walls. Georgie would understand...

'I'm so sorry, Dulcie.' Raff's hand came up, stroking the hair away from her face, tenderness in his touch. 'I'm not used to this...' And then his face darkened into a study of self-admonishment. 'But I *should* have seen it coming. Gus always had the press on his tail, and I know it wore him down sometimes...'

Blaming himself when it wasn't his fault, when he'd been so quick getting her inside, shielding her, protecting her, but he couldn't protect her from everything, from the fear and turmoil mounting inside. His touch was soothing, stirring a familiar ache. With her whole heart she wanted to lean into it, go with it, but if she did...

'Raff, I want to go home.'

His hand stilled. 'To England?'

She nodded.

And then the light was draining from his eyes. She closed hers so she didn't have to watch, so she could string some words together.

'I'm not what you need.' She felt tears burning behind her lids, an ache filling her throat. Maybe she was overreacting, but she couldn't help the way she was feeling, couldn't switch off the impulse to hide. 'I'm sorry. I care for you so much...' *more than you'll ever know* '...but I can't do this.'

There was a long, deep silence, and then he was removing his hand, stepping back. 'I understand.'

She felt her heart collapsing. Did he though? Could he see the tangle inside her, the fear and the anger, the hopelessness, and the love?

He breathed in audibly. 'The royal helicopter's your best bet if you want to avoid the press. It'll take you to the helipad at the Regal, or to the airport if you want. Barcelona, or Girona or Reus...' His voice was cracking now, putting cracks in her heart. 'I'll go prime the pilot.'

# CHAPTER FIFTEEN

*Six weeks later...*

'MORE CHAMPAGNE?'

Dulcie glanced at the bottle. She *wanted* more, yes, but she'd already had two top-ups, and getting any tipsier wouldn't do. She was on team bridesmaid, after all.

'No, thank you.' She smiled at the waiter, taking the opportunity to detach herself from the little group of guests she was with.

Mingling wasn't hard, nodding and smiling, framing the occasional interested exclamation, but it was dull. Even dissing those awful people from the past had felt pointless and boring. She looked over the lawn to where Georgie was standing, resplendent in ivory silk, looking every inch the perfect bride. Laughing with Peter, in love, glowing with it. Happiest day and all that. Georgie deserved nothing less.

She swallowed hard and headed for the shade.

It was tempting to sit down, but in spite of the warm sunshine there was a faint moisture clinging to the grass that would undoubtedly mark silk, and damp splotches were not a good look for a girl who'd already blotted her copybook by being photographed in only a dress shirt on the third deck of the Brostovenian royal yacht. So it was standing, nursing a half-empty glass, trying not to think about Raffiel, trying not to let the ache inside show.

She drew in a long breath. If only she could stop seeing that hope in his eyes, hope that there could be a future... Her stomach tightened. There couldn't be, of course, but it was still a torment, remembering. Those eyes. And his kiss. His touch. His smile. All the things she loved, missed, but the price was too high. She couldn't pay it, couldn't bear the scrutiny that would come if they were together. Just...*couldn't*!

She shook herself, lifted her glass to her lips. At least there was Fendlesham!

The sudden compulsion to return had come as a surprise. Maybe telling Raff about it had thrown it up her charts somehow, but, whatever, she was glad. Of course, because of the photographs she'd had some explaining to do to her parents, admitting the obvious, that she and Raff had had a thing, but she'd downplayed it, pretended it hadn't meant anything.

Maybe it had made her seem a bit wanton, but that was better than letting them conjure any fanciful notions. And then somehow, one explanation had led to another, and suddenly she'd been telling them all about Charlie, and it hadn't felt so hard because she'd already been through it with Raff. They'd been shocked, of course, horrified, angry, but she'd smoothed their fury down, then gone on to explain about Tommy. More horror, more sadness, but she'd told them she was fine, and she'd felt fine inside saying it, so it had to be true.

She looked up into the canopy. Leafy air. She breathed it in, pulling it all the way into her lungs. Yes, she *was* fine. Motivated actually. Brimming with energy. She felt a smile coming. She was Lady Dulcibella Davenport-Brown and she was making changes at Fendlesham. As she'd walked round the house and grounds, ideas for improvement had kept popping out. Pop, pop, pop! The counter in the café was in the wrong place. Moving it down would allow for six more covers. And the old stables were a total dead space, piled high with junk, coated in dust and dangling cobwebs. Clearing out the rubbish and removing some of the stalls would create an exhibition space, perfect for artists and makers. And the hayloft above could be converted into a mezzanine, which could be used for workshops…creative writing maybe, or felting. Whatever she could pull together. Because that was another thing she was going to do: create a programme of events that could provide extra year-round income, not a vast income, like the film location fees brought in, but enough to pay for bits of maintenance. For a start, the chimneys at the gate lodge were woefully in need of repointing!

Georgie seemed bemused by her schemes, but then Georgie could afford to be bemused. She wasn't inheriting a problem. Creighton Manor and all the work that went with it, was going to her older brother, Jonathan. Meanwhile Georgie was waltzing off into the sunset with Peter Harrington of the Harrington Bank group, waltzing off to an impeccable six-bedroom mansion in Kensington.

*Waltzing...*

Her heart dipped. That night, waltzing at The Imperial, the warmth of Raff's hand on her back, the way he'd held her, turned her, that heat in his gaze, desire pulsing through, the way his lips had found hers in the hotel lobby. She closed her eyes for a beat, fighting temptation, but it was no good. She set her glass down on the grass and took out her phone.

She couldn't be with Raffiel, couldn't share his public life, but at least his public life afforded her a glimpse. Hashtag Raffiel Munoz was the place the place she went in private, to torture herself. There were always new pictures trending. Raff at charity events, looking drop-dead gorgeous. Raff playing polo, managing somehow to look handsome in the helmet and—posted four hours ago—Raff boarding the royal jet, a burly body-guard at his heels. Off on some royal business, no doubt, probably hating it but smiling through anyway, for duty.

It was what she was doing too, smiling through for Georgie, mingling for Georgie, being the model bridesmaid for Georgie, not hating it, to be fair, but not exactly loving it either. She slipped her phone back and picked up her glass. *Enough.* Time for some cool sparkling water and more mind-numbing conversation with another group of total strangers!

'Ten minutes to landing, sir.'

'Thanks, Jed.'

He waited for his bodyguard to disappear then met his own eyes in the mirror, levelling the tails of his bow tie for the third time. Ridiculous how long it was taking to tie the damn thing.

*Come on, Raff, focus!*

Not so easy when his nerves were chiming, when the hopes he'd put through the shredder after Barcelona were busy gluing themselves back together.

He let his hands fall. What if Georgie was wrong? What if Dulcie wasn't obsessing over the management of Fendlesham to fill her miserable, heartbroken hours but was doing it for the love of home, a love he'd felt coming through from the moment she'd started describing it to him? And what if her sudden willingness to participate in social events, her willingness to talk and mingle with strangers, had nothing to do with proving herself worthy of her title, and of *him*, but was simply her finding her feet again, building on the experience of Barcelona with the 'hens' who became 'girls' and then friends…?

It wasn't as if keeping a busy schedule himself had anything to do with Dulcie, or, at least, anything to do with framing a future for the two of them. Yes, successive royal duties did help to keep his mind from sliding backwards, and the evening hours he was putting in compiling a dossier about his country—GDP, resources, taxation, debt, infrastructure, population distribution—did help to keep the pain ghosts at bay, but if he was getting on with life, trying to do his best, trying to take the weight off Papa, then why couldn't it be that Dulcie was doing the same thing, helping to take the weight off her own parents, coming into her own, for herself?

But Georgie was adamant and…determined! God knows how she'd acquired his secretary's number, but somehow she had, and then Karolina had been putting through the call, and Georgie had been berating him roundly for not being straight with Dulcie from the start, for putting her poor cousin through hell, and then her tone had suddenly shaded into concern, her love for Dulcie shining through.

*'Do you love her, Raff?'*

He'd felt the pain surfacing then, catching him in the chest and throat.

*'Yes, I do, but she wants to live a private life, Georgie, and I must respect that, because I know how precious it is. I was free and now I'm not. I had no choice, but Dulcie does, and I won't try to persuade her to a life I don't even want myself.'*

*'That's very noble, I must say, but here's the thing: my shy, introvert cousin is on fire right now. She's drowning in schemes, refits, and renovations. She's planning a ceramics exhibition, workshops. "You know, Georgie, we've got outbuildings to spare so why not use them, create new streams of revenue...?" She's relishing it all so hard, Raff, that I can't help thinking that what's really going on is that she's compensating, or she's on a mission to prove herself somehow, and the only reason that comes to mind is that deep down, subconsciously, it's all for you.'*

Georgie had paused then.

*'She's in love with you, Raff. I knew it in Bar-*

*celona, and I know it now. So the way I see it,
if you love her and she loves you, then you can
work it out. Come to my wedding, see her, talk
to her. Please, Raff...'*

He'd said no, told Georgie it wouldn't be fair.

God, even on the yacht, when his heart had
been breaking, screaming at him to tell Dulcie
he was in love with her, use his feelings to stop
her from leaving, he'd resisted because she'd
looked so small and broken standing there with
the past surfacing in her eyes, everything she'd
been through with Charlie, the cruel exposure,
that frustrated helplessness. In that moment he'd
known categorically that whatever he was feeling, he couldn't use love as a weapon, so instead
he'd pushed his pain down and steeled himself
to be strong for her, organising the helicopter so
she could escape.

But Georgie must have steeled herself too, for
victory. For the past two weeks she'd been the
voice in his ear, feeding him hope, stirring his
feelings so hard that now he couldn't even get
his fingers to work, working on him so relentlessly that now, somehow, he was on the royal
jet, on his way to her Oxfordshire wedding re-
ception, the plus one Dulcie didn't know she had.
His stomach roiled. What was waiting for him?
Happiness or heartbreak?

'Sir...?'

Jed again. All one hundred and seventy pounds of him.

'The pilot says you need to take your seat for landing.'

'Thanks.' He sucked in a breath and attacked the tie again, working it into a passable bow, giving it a final tug. 'I'm coming.'

Dulcie scanned the seating plan, felt her heart sinking. Why on earth had Georgie marooned her on a table with a collection of Peter's elderly relatives? Nancy, Edward, Posey, Crispin, Henry, Harriet, and JJ. She hadn't come across JJ yet, but she'd attempted a conversation with Posey in the garden earlier. It had been a bit of a comedy show since Posey was hard of hearing. Come to think of it, so were Great-Uncle Crispin and Great-Aunt Harriet. As for Great-Uncle Henry, he was likely to spend the entire dinner asleep because he'd been sozzled and swaying when he'd passed her not twenty minutes ago. She eyed a passing tray of champagne. Maybe getting sozzled was the right idea!

'Excuse me, Lady Davenport-Brown…?'

'Yes…' She turned. It was Felix, Lord Rayner's butler.

Felix inclined his head, leaning in. 'I'm sorry to disturb you but Jasper Júlio has arrived…?'

'Jasper Jú—'

Her breath stopped. And then her limbs were turning to rubber. JJ! *Raffiel!* Here? But how? Why? And then an unexpected sob arrived, thickening in her throat, straining at her chest. *Georgie!* She was behind this. It had *her* finger-prints all over it. That extra little twinkle going on in Georgie's eyes every time she'd looked over. She'd put it down to their reclaimed close-ness, to wedding-day sparkle, but it wasn't. It was this...this plan hatched in secret... Oh, God! And Raff had colluded, was here. *Here!*

'Are you all right, madam?'

No. She most definitely wasn't *all right*. What to think? What to feel? How to pin a single thought down when her blood was rushing, and her heart was thrashing, and tears were burn-ing. She swallowed hard. But she *must* think. Because Raff was here and it had to mean he wanted them to try, wanted *her* to try. Could she? Could she let go of her fear—for him—so she could *be* with him instead of missing him every second of every day? Oh, God, just the thought of him, those eyes, those lips, those strong arms, the safety inside them...

She felt her breath slowing. Because that was how he'd always made her feel, wasn't it? Safe. Protected. It was why she'd been able to open herself up to him, letting out all the hurt that had been dragging her down, cramping her style, and she was stronger for it, steadier. And that steadiness had given her the courage to open up to her parents, let them in again, and it had cleared space in her head and in her heart, space she'd been able to devote to her beloved Fendlesham. She was pulling her weight, doing her bit, and she'd been doing her bit at this wedding too, circulating, mingling, not loving it, but the thing was she *could* do it, was *doing* it, and, with Raff by her side, maybe she could do it better, come not to dread it, and maybe having *her* by his side would help him too, help him face what was coming.

*Could...* It was a word full of possibilities, the key to a world of possibilities. She felt a little lightness coming. And the thing was, she was wiser now, and so was Raff. No more forgetting that the press could be lurking. Knowing the enemy was half the battle. The other half was knowing...

She drew in a breath, refocusing. 'Yes Felix, I'm absolutely fine, thank you, maybe even better than fine.' She felt a smile loosening, a tingle winding through. 'So, tell me, where will I find Jasper Júlio?'

'He's in the library, madam.'

Raffiel ran his finger around his collar. It wasn't tight, just felt tight, as did his throat, and his chest for that matter. *Nerves!*

He turned away from the window, ran his eyes over the polished furniture and the leatherbound volumes lining the walls, only half taking them in. Maybe *Jasper Júlio* would make her smile. It had seemed like a good way to forewarn her, because no way had he been going to just walk up to her in front of everyone. She'd have hated that, being on display *again*. Because of him, she'd been on display quite enough already, in the hall of columns, in the lobby of The Imperial and—he felt his stomach shrinking—worst of all, on the royal yacht.

No, there'd be no public sighting of the two of them at this wedding or anywhere else until…his heart quivered…*unless* it was what she wanted. He felt sweat breaking along his hairline. Would it be what she wanted? Georgie thought so but that didn't mean—

The door creaked, yanking him round, yanking his breath away.

'Jasper Julio, I presume…?'

Blue eyes gleaming, a smile tucked into the corners of her luscious mouth. Her dress was pale green silk, and…she was wearing his necklace.

He felt his heart filling, a smile rising. 'The one and only.'

'How fortuitous.' She closed the door then stepped into the room, smiling that mischievous smile of hers.

'How so?'

She was coming nearer, sighing. 'Well, the thing is I have an ache that won't go away.'

'A spinal thing?' He took two tingling steps, stopping in front of her.

'No.' And then suddenly tears were mounting from her lower lids, glistening. 'It's more of a heart thing.'

He held his breath, or maybe it was that he didn't dare to breathe.

'It's a full-on love thing, to be honest. Been going on for ages.'

So Georgie was right.

He felt a hot ache filling his throat. 'Ages…?'

How was it possible to be feeling so many things in the space of a single heartbeat? Joy, relief, and this huge vibrating ball of pure, bright, overwhelming love.

He had to touch her, take her face into his hands. 'Ages, as in from the very first moment? Because that's how long I've had it…'

Her eyes closed as if she was savouring the words, and then she was looking at him again, stealing his breath, his heart, his soul. 'You love me?'

'Oh, Dulce, why else would I be here? I love you with every breath in my body.' Tears were escaping from her eyes now, rolling down her cheeks. He caught them with his thumbs, feeling a scald behind his own lids. 'I wanted to tell you that day on the yacht, but I didn't because I didn't want it to feel like pressure…'

'Oh, Raff, are you for real?' And then she was smiling, wet-eyed. 'I wanted to say it too, so many times, but I was too scared, because love at first sight is mad, right, like a total fairy tale?' And then her smile faded a little. 'So, what happens now?'

Eyes to drown in, that sweet mouth he needed to claim, taste, explore.

'I think we kiss, and then…' He brushed his lips over hers, feeling the familiar pulse spike and a swell of pure, overwhelming happiness. 'Then in true fairy-tale tradition, I think we live happily ever after.'

'Mmm…' He felt her lips curving under his, her cheeks lifting. 'I like the sound of that…'

# EPILOGUE

*Breaking: King Raffiel Munoz*
*marries Barcelona lover*
*Lady Dulcibella Davenport-Brown!*

AFTER CAUSING A *stir with their passionate antics in the lobby of The Imperial Hotel, at the Architects Against Homelessness Charity Ball in Barcelona last year, King Raffiel Munoz of Brostovenia and Lady Dulcibella Davenport-Brown tied the knot today in a lavish ceremony at the English bride's family seat, Fendlesham Hall.*

*For a Brostovenian king to marry outside his own country is a significant break with tradition, but in a press statement issued two days before the wedding, King Raffiel was determinedly unapologetic.*

*He said, 'Fendlesham is dear to my fiancée, and my fiancée is dear to me. I don't care where I marry her, as long as I marry her.'*

*King Raffiel has been quick to establish his*

*own style of monarchy, so this particular departure from tradition is very much in keeping.*

*The marriage ceremony was not broadcast live, but has been recorded for future release. There will, however, be some official photographs released later today.*

*The bride's dress, designed by Lady Dulcibella's cousin, Lady Georgina Rayner Harrington, is rumoured to be breathtaking.*

\* \* \* \* \*

*If you enjoyed this story, check out these other great reads from Ella Hayes*

**Their Surprise Safari Reunion**
**The Single Dad's Christmas Proposal**
**Tycoon's Unexpected Caribbean Fling**
**Unlocking the Tycoon's Heart**

*All available now!*